THE Naughty WEEK

USA TODAY BESTSELLING AUTHOR
JADE WEST

The Naughty Week © 2025 Jade West

The moral rights of the author have been asserted.

All rights reserved. No part of this publication may be reproduced, distributed, or transmitted in any form or by any means, including photocopying, recording, or other electronic or mechanical methods, without the prior written permission of the publisher, except in the case of brief quotations embodied in critical reviews and certain other non-commercial uses permitted by copyright law. For permission requests, write to the publisher, addressed "Attention: Permissions Coordinator," at the email address below.

Cover design by RBA Designs
Interior formatting by Sammi Bee
Edited by John Hudspith www.johnhudspith.co.uk
All enquiries to pa@jadewestauthor.co.uk

*To all of the keen hardcorers out there... I hope you enjoy this filth-filled vacation.
I sure did.*

one

I have no idea how I managed to pack so much for a week in Cannes, considering that the bulk of my luggage is nothing more than fancy underwear and flipflops. I haven't even packed any toys, since Heath assured us he's already stocked up to the max. No metal butt plugs to be worried about showing up on the airport scanners at least.

Not that I'd be all that embarrassed if they did.

My days of reservations and hangups are long behind me. Sex is an open book for me now. It's my favourite hobby, not just my career, and I'm happy to admit it to virtually anyone – even airport security if it came to it. Having especially filthy fun while I'm earning heaps of cash as an *entertainer* is nothing but a massive cherry on top.

I'm exceptionally lucky that I'll be having two very luscious cherries on top of me this week, and one of them is awaiting us at his swanky villa right now.

The other cherry is right here, beside me.

Josh, my stunner of a boyfriend, hoists our hand luggage into the compartments over our heads. His t-shirt has ridden up just enough to see the V of his hips and the dark promise of hair down his stomach. He gets more ripped by the week, I swear it. His six pack will have a six pack at this rate.

"Excited?" he asks, once he's buckled up in the seat beside me.

"You could say that, yeah. Just a teensy bit. Who wouldn't love a trip to Cannes? Sun, sea, sex… and a host to die for. It's going to be amazing."

Josh nudges my foot with his. "Keep it down," he says and I have to laugh. Our client confidentiality comes at all costs given we're high-class Agency performers, but seriously, I'm hardly going to scream that we're off for a week of hardcore paid sex with one of the hottest TV stars on the planet, am I?

As much as I'd like to.

I look around the cabin, at the people going about their business, flying away on holiday, just like we are. None of them have any idea we're being paid a token grand each for the honour of a week-long filth fest with the famous Heath Mason from Nighttime Whispers.

I'd love to scream it over the tannoy. I'd jump up and down as I shared the news that I'll be getting Heath's dick for seven days straight and enjoying the French Riviera as a bonus.

"Oh, and did you know, folks? He's even got a Jacob's ladder!"

I grin to myself. A whole load of people on this flight will be fans of the show, just like me. They'd probably give us a round of applause for getting the chance at seven full days with Heath. I remember when he was just a TV idol to me, before Josh took me on a joint *proposal* that practically knocked me off my feet. How he ever kept it a secret that the man we watched onscreen together was a client of his is commendable. Such a professional.

And we'll both be professionals this week. That's what comes first.

This isn't just a holiday. It's a work trip. We are going to Cannes to please Heath, first and foremost. His wish is our command, literally.

I have to remember that. The lines can't afford to get blurry – not in this industry, and Heath Mason is particularly guarded. His walls of anonymity are sky high in comparison to my tumbling lows.

Heath has no pseudonym, like I do. He's the famous Heath Mason, instantly recognisable from a mile away, but I'm Holly the whore when I'm working, and sweet Ella Edwards when I'm not.

My ex, Connor never revealed the real identity of the hooker love of his life who broke his soul. How considerate of him.

Yeah, right.

Connor is the most selfish prick I know. He only kept my identity a secret because he knew I'd call his lies out as utter bullshit. Cheating asshole.

I love flying. I'm transfixed when the plane rumbles down the runway and begins our ascent into the sky. I've got the window seat and watch as the UK disappears underneath us. Here we go. Up, up and away.

I'm so caught up with the view that it takes me a minute to register just how intently Josh is staring at me.

"What?" I ask him, and he leans over to give me a kiss on the temple.

"Nothing. Just admiring my gothic goddess."

I'm hardly at my gothic height today in a black cami dress and simple black sandals, but I have still got my regular catflicks and scarlet red lipstick on.

"I'm not the only goth you'll be admiring today, my sweet prince," I reply, and Josh gives my foot another nudge with his. The tension in his brows makes me giggle.

"Fine!" I say, and pretend to zip my mouth up, with a roll of my eyes.

Heath Mason, our glamourous client, rivals me in the goth stakes, which is no surprise since he plays a vampire for a living. His long hair is as black as mine, and his eyes are as pale a blue as mine are. He was born for Nighttime Whispers. They couldn't have possibly cast anyone better for the show.

It's only going to be a short flight before we land in Cannes and get to see him in person. We usually see him once a fortnight, on joint proposals, but it's been four weeks this time, due to his filming schedule, and boy, do I know it. I've felt those extra two weeks more than I imagined, and so has Josh. He even suggested binge watching season one of Nighttime Whispers a few nights ago, which is unheard of. I'm normally the one who flicks straight to the show when it's on.

I may be a fan of NW, but Josh is more of a fan of the man himself. If you could call it that. He's been a client of Heath's for years, and from the moment I saw them greet each other I knew there was a bond that runs far deeper than a fortnightly paycheck ever will.

That's one of the things that makes the experiences between the three of us so powerful. No matter how many times we see Heath, the intensity blows my mind. I doubt that will ever change, either. You could never extinguish a flame that bright. Distance only makes it burn brighter.

I feel Josh's foot tapping to a rhythm beside me.

"You alright?" I ask him. "Getting flight nerves?"

"It's not nerves I'm feeling, it's… excitement."

"Yeah, I'm buzzing, too. Can't wait to hit Cannes, and watch the clouds on the way, just woah. Perfect."

Josh's gorgeous green eyes dig into mine, and he squeezes my knee.

"I couldn't give a shit about clouds. I'm talking *excitement*, excitement. Right now."

I look at him blankly until he grins and jerks his head towards the toilet at the end of the aisle.

"Are you for real?" I ask. "We'll be touching down in less than an hour, I'm sure you can wait a bit before you explode in your pants."

He rolls his eyes, and I realise how loud my voice is. Damn. I'm losing my filter more and more each day. I blame Tiffany, Josh's best friend, and the most hardcore entertainer at The Agency. She has a voice like a megaphone and a cackle that could shake the plane.

Josh leans in. "Yes, I'm sure I could wait a bit before I explode in my pants, but I don't want to. I want to take advantage of the opportunity."

"The opportunity? For what?" I whisper. "It's not as though we haven't plane fucked before." I flutter my eyelashes. "Are my sandals driving you crazy or something?"

"No," he says. "*You* are. And this is the last opportunity for me to get you all to myself before arrival. I'm not going to miss it."

"Jeez," I say, "is that a bit of possessiveness I hear? It gives me flutters to know how much a guy like you wants a girl like me."

"Oh, I want you so bad right now," he says, and the lust in his eyes sends my temperature soaring.

"And let me make it irresistible for you," he says, "I noticed, when we were boarding, that this plane's toilets have a window."

"Yeah? Really?"

"Yes, really. It'll be a tight fit, in more ways than one, but you can cloud gaze till your heart's content while I fill you up from behind."

"How sweet of you."

My butterflies for Josh never die down, no matter how much time we spend together. I take a look at the bulge in his jeans as he rises from his seat, and have to clench my thighs, because suddenly I want him so bad.

It's his voice, his eyes, his touch, his huge, pierced dick and the way he's such a master at using it. It's everything about the man.

"Three minutes," he leans down to whisper. "I'll be waiting."

I never get tired of being *naughty*. I watch him as he walks away down the aisle, already pulsing with need for him.

My heart is racing once the three minutes are up and I head

after him. I have a smile on my face, trying to stay calm and nonchalant as I step closer and closer towards my waiting boyfriend. The toilet to the right has *engaged* on it. I tap lightly on the door and it swings open. Josh pulls me inside and bolts it up again like it's a Venus fly trap, and he's straight on me, his hot lips on mine as he clamps my hand around his swollen cock, working it up and down. The barbells feel so good under his skin. All six of them. They make me clench up at the thought of them pushing inside me.

And for one whole week, I'm going to have two steel ladders pushing wherever the hell they feel like.

I kiss Josh back, enjoying the way his pierced tongue dances with mine, but my pussy is already desperate for the monster in my grip.

"Enough," Josh says and turns to me to face the window.

He wasn't wrong about it being a tight fit. I'm practically squashed up and star-fished, bracing my arms against the walls, but fuck, the view out of the little oval window is amazing, a blanket of clouds down below and a bright blue sky.

Almost as amazing as having my panties wrenched to one side and the head of his monster cock opening me up.

"Ready, baby?"

"Always," I tell him.

"No screaming," he says and pushes in past the first bar, the nip and pull on my pussy enough to make me groan.

"Quiet!" he says and pushes all the way, ping after ping as the ladder impales me.

And holy fucking shit it feels so good, full to the brim with my boyfriend's incredible cock, my breath fogging the window.

"You good?" he asks.

"More than good," I tell him. "Get me fucked... please."

"I thought I was the one who was desperate for a plane fuck," he says. "You're always a horny little bitch, Ells. You'd take every cock on offer in this plane and still be wet for more."

Josh's filthy mouth makes me feel so slutty.

"Yeah, I would. But you're the only one who gets my pussy for free."

"And you're the one who gets this for free, so enjoy it, you kinky little mantrap."

He pulls his cock out by three bars, his standard starting move, and I love it when he slides back in. I'm so wet it fucking squelches.

I'm grinning like a doped-up bitch when he gets into a rhythm. I'd give anything for a good hard slamming right now, but no. I grit my teeth and take it, savouring the heat as my pussy grips him.

He picks up the pace and his hands find my tits, squeezing hard as he pounds me.

Fuck yes. And fuck the clouds. I drop my head, and one hand, and somehow manage to find my clit.

I strum it like a mad bitch and my boyfriend pauses, his cock halfway out.

I know what's coming – both of us.

He drives back in and I nip my clit and he fucks me fast. And I'm done. Shuddering and biting off a long moan as my pussy pulsates around his onslaught.

"Fuck," he says and I take the slam without a yell, gritting my teeth as he pumps his cum into me.

When he's done, he helps me to stand. I shuffle around and drop myself onto the toilet for a pee, his cum dribbling out of me.

"That was amazing," I tell him.

His cock is still dripping juice and cum, so I give it a suck to clean him up.

"Thanks, baby," he says, before he shoves it back into his pants, and I'm done too. I give myself a good wipe before I wriggle back into my panties and straighten down my dress, and we're back to it. Just two regular travellers ready for the beauty of Cannes.

Or more specifically, the beauty of the man waiting for us.

Josh's crotch is already bulging again by the time we get back to our seats, coast clear, and my pussy is already throbbing for more. Damnit. Will my sex drive ever stop rising?

We give each other a dirty smile and his hand squeezes mine in silent acknowledgement.

This holiday is going to be one hell of a ride.

Touchdown can't come soon enough, and neither can I.

two

My excitement ramps up to a whole other level once our feet hit the ground in Cannes. The airport is buzzing, and I feel like a kid at a fairground as I take Josh's hand – practically bouncing along at his side to get our luggage. The warmth of the French sun bathes us in pure bliss when we step outside to find our driver waiting, holding up a *Josh and Ella* sign. I want to dash on over with a squeal, but Josh squeezes my hand a little tighter.

"Relax. We're just regular holidaymakers, remember?"

I stare up at him through my sunglasses, admiring how hot he looks in his. He's like a secret agent when it comes to anonymity, and an uber professional when it comes to playing it cool. He's so concerned for Heath's privacy that it radiates from him hotter than the sun.

That's it. Of course it is. His main driving factor right now.

He's protective of Heath.

"Relax?" I say. "Regular holidaymakers can be out of their minds with excitement, no? So come on, show you're excited, just a little. It'll look weirder if you're not."

He smiles at that, and I've got him. He's buzzing just as hard as I am, he's just got a thicker shell, and it's actually a great thing to see. I love the protective side of Josh. I love how determined he is to protect the people close to him at all costs.

"Ok. You're right," he says. "Kudos to you for the rationale. Go on, Ella. Let rip. We're happy holidaymakers, after all."

"Let's go!" I say, and with that I wheel my case at lightning speed towards the waiting car, giggling all the way.

Heath has kept it low key with the transport. The driver is friendly with a suave *bonjour* as he lugs our cases into the back, and his car is great, but it's hardly a limo with blacked out windows. It's just a cab, ready to take us to a flash villa that could belong to anyone.

Who cares who that *anyone* happens to be?

I catch sight of the sea on the way there, pointing it out to Josh with fervour.

"I love the sea," I tell him. "It's one of my favourite things, you know? Sandy beaches, and ocean waves. Drives me crazy."

"Yes. I do know. And moonlight shining down as they crash." Josh's smirk rises on one side. "It's *amazing*, I know. Just bear in mind, we might not make it there. Not this time. We might be too busy."

"Spoilsport," I laugh. "I hope I get to at least dip my toes."

I'm grinning wide when our final destination comes into view up ahead. The huge gates swing open automatically and the cab pulls into the driveway, and woah... this place. Heath's villa is nothing like the gothic paradise he's constructed out of bricks and mortar back in London. There are no black edged windows, or gothic archways, and no dark gravel lining the driveway. This is one of those white, square, modern wonders of a construction – three storeys high with balconies and terraces on every floor. And huge windows. So many huge windows!

I raise my sunglasses and give a *wow* as the cab leaves and the gates close behind it, blocking the view of the road. The huge floor to ceiling windows of the villa's second floor reflect the sun beautifully, and I just about get sight of an infinity pool, glowing pastel blue. It must look right out onto the sea, I can see it from here.

And that's not surprising, seeing as the villa itself is just a stone's throw away from it... a few small steps from Heath's place onto the sandy shore.

Who knows? Maybe I will get the sand under my feet. Even for just one token dash across the beach.

"This is gorgeous," I say to Josh. "Absolutely fucking gorgeous."

"Just like it's owner." Josh is looking around, scouting the place, but he isn't admiring the infinity pool, or the closeness of the beach like I am, he's scoping out the perimeter. A tall hedge lines the border, and the windows are reflective. Nobody will be staring in.

With that, I hear the front door open, and our host yells *Welcome to Paradise!*

My heart leaps when my eyes land on Heath, because his beauty puts the surroundings to shame. Even though he's barefoot in a plain black t-shirt and shorts, with his hair scooped up into a messy bun, he knocks the breath right out of my lungs.

It's Josh who steps forward first, holding out a hand before Heath pulls him in for a hug. You'd think they were long term buddies from the outside, with a *hey, great to see you!* But they hold each other too tightly for college friends – pressed chest to chest and swaying together just a little too long.

Then it's my turn.

"Hello, my darling *curva*," Heath says, with a dashing smile, and my legs feel bandy as he pulls me close.

Curva is my pet name now, playing on Heath's vamp character's native tongue. Curva means slut, and I'll be his darling *curva* any day of the week, which works just great considering I am going to be his darling *curva* every single day of this one.

Heath takes my case as Josh takes his, and even though this villa is a completely new environment to me, I'm feeling relaxed from the moment we step over the threshold.

Heath's character screams loud, even though the villa is neutral cream and airy in decor. He has a few black abstract pieces of art up on the walls, sure, and a humorous black gloss voodoo doll knife block on the kitchen counter. But more than that, it's him. He doesn't need the decor to radiate his personality through the building, his energy does that all on its own.

"Lunchtime drinks?" he asks. "Beer and lime?"

He knows we like those.

I lean on his countertop as he gets our drinks, and we raise them in *cheers* for our first toast of the day.

"How was your flight?" he asks, and I blurt the truth right out.

"Josh fucked me in the toilet on the plane because he couldn't keep his dick in his pants. I must have looked like a weirdo starfish with my face pressed up to the window."

Heath laughs before he wags a finger at Josh.

"One load of cum down before you even arrive? Tut tut. I hope I don't have to chastise you for it later."

"As if." Josh laughs. "One load down isn't going to hurt anyone. I'm sure Ella's still a mess in her panties, so you can call it a warmup in your favour. Or *flavour*."

The pair of them look at me and I have to giggle as I roll my eyes.

"Jeez, guys. We haven't even unpacked yet and we're already hot on the thought of cummy panties."

The zing in the air is so strong, it's crackling, and it still splits me into two fluttery halves when it comes to our extravagant client. On one hand, Heath is my celebrity crush, fast becoming a good friend of mine. I want to hug him, and fawn like a fangirl as I ask him questions about Nighttime Whispers all night long, but on the other hand, I'm already desperate for the depths of pure and utter filth we'll be offering him. And that I know he'll be demanding...

"Talking of unpacking, let me give you a tour of the abode,"

Heath says, and I almost want to reply with a *fuck no, tear my cum-stained panties off me!*

"But first," he says and holds out his hands. "I'll need your phones and passports, please. Privacy at all costs. I'm sure you won't ever want to oust me, but random holiday snaps could cause a whole host of problems. I'll be putting my phone away as well."

I don't give it a second thought before I dig in my bag for my phone and passport, and neither does Josh. We hand them over and Heath opens a cupboard to the side of the fridge, nothing obvious, but it holds a safe inside. Good spot for one. Nobody would ever know.

He puts our belongings inside and locks up, greeting us with another broad smile – and a dirty look in his eyes.

"Since you are *clients* here for your break, as well as welcome guests, I've come up with some surprises for you. I hope you'll enjoy them as much as I will."

"Surprises?" Josh asks.

"Yes. Surprises. Dirty surprises."

"Come on, spill the beans," my boyfriend laughs. "Don't be a tease. This isn't Nighttime Whispers, ending on a cliffhanger."

Heath shakes his head.

"All will be revealed when it's time. But first, the tour. Let me show you your home for the week."

Home.

Strangely, it already feels like it.

Heath is a proud man as he shows us around, room to room. The villa is deluxe and open plan in the main, but it has a separate cinema lounge where the whole damn wall is a TV screen. It would be outright perfect for some Nighttime Whispers, and some more… intimate viewings. Imagine an up-close shot of double anal on that thing. What a vision.

Heath laughs as he catches my smirk. I waggle my eyebrows and lick my lips as I point to the screen.

"Yes, yes, I know," he says. "I've used this screen for plenty of filthy fun, Ella. I'm sure you'll get the pleasure of experiencing it."

"Sounds good to me."

"I'm certain you'll get the pleasure of experiencing a whole variety of things here, so come on, let's keep going."

Holy shit, Heath's terraces are absolutely phenomenal, especially the one by the infinity pool. It catches the sun like a dream, and the tall hedge below means we'll be away from any prying eyes. He picked this spot for a reason, that much is obvious.

The three of us finish up our beers together, leaning over the railings and admiring the view of the shore.

"There's a gate down there." Heath points to the far corner of the gardens. "It's security locked, but leads just across a path, down to the beach. Practically private, since we're the last in the row."

Josh squeezes my shoulder as I strain for a view. "Ah, so maybe you'll get some sand between your toes after all."

"Or sand between your legs," Heath says. "But we shouldn't. *I* shouldn't. The paps would have a fucking field day. Maybe I'll allow you some time out of your whoring duties to take a private stroll. It's no bearing on me what my guests choose to get up to."

I'd love to get naked and frolic on the beach with Josh, playing naked in the sea, but my heart drops a little at the thought Heath won't be there to join us. For Josh as well as me. Josh would love filthy fun with all three of us down there, just us much as I would. I'm still pondering the thought when Heath claps his hands.

"On to the bedrooms," he says, and leads us to the top floor. "There are five guest rooms to choose from, so pick whichever takes your fancy." He pauses with a twinkle in his bright blue eyes – his vampire smirk to die for when he opens the door at the far end. "Or you can always feel free to use mine. Come take a look."

I step past my vampire crush into his bedroom to find that it's another cream beauty of open space, with an absolutely enormous bed, big enough for at least twenty people at once.

"Wow," I say.

"Fucking ditto," Josh says.

Heath laughs. "Indeed. It's handmade, carved from solid oak. And the mattress itself is a work of art. We had to remove the windows to crane the thing in here. As you will soon discover, it's like fucking on a cloud."

There's a single black piece of poured art hanging in place over the iron railed headboard, and black lamps on either side of the bed, but that's all for *goth* in here. I can see into his ensuite, and the bathtub is built into the floor, so big it's almost a mini pool. Jesus fucking Christ, what a pad.

I do a twirl as I check it out. "Umm… I think I know which room I'd prefer to hole up in, how about you, Joshua?"

Josh has his arms folded, leaning back against the wall as he grins.

"As if that's even a question." He looks at Heath. "I'm glad you offered. This way you'll be prepared for our company, rather than have us gatecrash unexpectedly in the middle of the night."

"It's set, then?" I ask. "We're staying in this one? All three of us?"

I still can't believe the fact that I'm on holiday with two barbell dicked gods. I remember the excitement of being a kid going to the beach with my parents, jumping up and down with my bucket and spade in my hands. That was off the scale, but holy shit. The full whammy of the week ahead hits me.

We are in Cannes! In a luxury villa! With Heath fucking Mason!

And we're sharing his ridiculous bed as well as his cock. Do holiday excursions ever get as exciting as this one? I doubt it.

Heath is watching me as well as Josh is. Two gorgeous guys checking me out as I dash over to the windows for another view of the sea. There it is, in sparkling brilliance. Fuck me, I'm a lucky girl.

"This is amazing," I say. "Seriously, guys, this is absolutely amazing." I turn to lock eyes with our client. Our host. *Heath.* "Thank you so much for having us."

"You are more than welcome," Heath says. "And as for having you, I can't stop thinking about the cum stained panties between those gorgeous thighs." His eyes move to his bed and then back to mine – his icy stare making me flutter. "Get up on there now, *sweet curva,* and show me the filthy leftovers."

three

It's a pleasure to climb up onto Heath's deluxe bed and spread my sweaty thighs for him. Such a filthy crotch on such clean cotton sheets. I lie back with a smile on my face, rubbing my fingers up and down my slit through my panties. Fuck, it's amazing to see the way the guys are staring at me. Josh looks proud of the mess he'll have made, and Heath licks his lips – no doubt as keen for a taste of Josh's leftovers as he is for a taste of my pussy.

I love that about him. I adore the way he adores Josh.

I kick off my sandals and hitch my legs higher, lolling open my thighs even wider and tugging the cum stained lace tight between my pussy lips. It feels so nice against my clit as I grind the fabric back and forth. I'm already heady when the guys approach. I watch with horny glee as Heath kisses my boyfriend with fervour. They tear each other's clothes off until they're dick to dick – both cocks glistening hard and proud.

I'll never tire of watching two Jacob's ladders in action together. They are absolutely fucking beautiful, just like the men they belong to.

I have to slow down my efforts, or I'll come from the sight of them. I groan as I stop teasing my clit with the fabric, panting as I imagine what is lying ahead.

From the way Heath is acting with Josh, it's obvious he's too desperate for a long warmup. I can see it in his eyes when he pulls away from Josh and stares at me instead.

"Off with that dress, curva, I'm desperate for a sight of those stunning tits of yours."

"So am I," Josh adds.

"Just leave those dirty panties on," Heath says. "I want to see the full extent of what I missed out on earlier."

"My pleasure."

I shimmy my cami dress up and over my head, tossing it off the bed before I take off my bra as well. I hold my tits together, showing off the size of them before tugging at my nipples. I'm very blessed in that department. Huge tits with pretty, pert nipples that my clients always go crazy for. Oh, how I want two pairs of rough hands on them right now. Pinching and grabbing. Two mouths, nipping and sucking.

Both men climb up beside me, and I get the first taste of Heath's lips on mine as Josh palms my tits, mashing them tight. I can't help but tug Heath's hair free from its bun, adoring the way it tumbles. I run my fingers through it and meet his eyes. I hold his face as I kiss him, still struggling to comprehend the fact that this is the man I've been watching onscreen for years.

"I've missed you both so much," he says as he breaks the kiss.

"Yeah, and we've missed you, too," I reply. "Haven't we, Josh?"

"Kind of, yeah. You could say that. I've missed your dirty ass in particular. One of a kind."

"Same goes." Heath smirks. "But I've also missed these."

My idol lowers his mouth and grazes his lips across one of my hard nipples. I raise my hands above my head and moan, my flesh screaming out for him.

"So beautiful," he says, and sucks on one of my tits, swirling his gorgeous tongue. His mouth is so wide, and so fucking wet. So hungry.

"You're making me jealous," Josh says and takes the other side, both guys feasting on my tits like I'm a banquet.

I'm already squirming when their teeth start nipping me. I'm panting as they grip my tits as well as suck, using me just the way I like it. I think it's Josh's hand that snakes down and tugs the lace taut between my pussy lips, mimicking the motions I was making myself. My God, it's fucking amazing.

"The scent of your cunt is irresistible," Heath says as Josh works me up.

The filthy vampire's beauty gives me crazy butterflies as he lowers himself between my legs.

"Such a gorgeous creature, you dirty *curva*," he says with a smile, and Josh moves his hand away to let Heath splay my pussy lips around my panties. He swipes his tongue across the fabric, and Josh joins him, up close.

"How does it taste?" Josh asks him.

"Delicious," Heath says, and sucks my clit through the lace with a groan. "Creamy panties. Such a treasure. Now, let's make them even creamier."

He tugs them down enough to push two fingers inside me, both covered in fabric. He digs around my cunt, and I imagine Josh's cum still in there, being soaked up. Heath gasps as he pulls his fingers free, and he must have found treasure. I raise myself on my elbows to watch him lapping at the lace, and he does it again – more juice, more cum.

"Your turn," he says to Josh, taking him by the hair. He guides my boyfriend's open mouth towards my pussy, and Josh shoots me a filthy smirk as he takes up where Heath left off, sucking and lapping at the sopping lace.

They take it in turns, over and over, driving the lace in and out, and cleaning up the spillage. And then they share, truly. Two hungry mouths kissing and sucking, tasting the dirtiness between my legs. Two hot guys, hands in each other's hair as they kiss and bite. Holy fuck, the pleasures never end.

They take a break from making out and Josh finally tugs my panties off me to reveal my naked slit. I slide my fingers down and hook two inside, horny for a taste myself. But there is no cum left now, just a faint taste of Josh's leftovers.

Heath sees me do it, and his smile lights up his icy eyes.

"Keep your fingers to yourself, curva. We're not done yet."

He sweeps his tongue across my clit, and it's my fingers in his hair now as he works his magic with my pussy, naked and bare without my panties. He sucks and laps, and I hold his head to me, squirming. Fuck, how I've missed this. Missed *him.*

"Sharing is caring, remember?" Josh says, and I groan as Heath moves aside. I need them both so bad.

Josh's tongue piercing makes me gasp when it hits my clit – just like always. I hold my boyfriend's head to me instead, trying to buck and grind to tip myself over the edge, but Josh is too skilled to let me come so easily. He only gives me the very tip of his tongue in tiny flicks with no fucking rhythm.

"Please," I say, but he looks up at me with devilment in his eyes.

"Not yet, baby. It's Heath's party. He deserves another taste."

They keep switching, the bastards, bringing me to the peak, then easing off. Heath laps and sucks until I start panting, and then Josh takes over, keeping me right on the edge of the crest before handing me back over. They are so skilled, so hot, playing my pussy like an instrument until I'm practically delirious, groaning with the need to come.

It's Heath's mouth that finally gives me the honour, pushing two fingers inside me as he sucks. My fingers are back in his hair when I come, my heels up on the perfect cloud of his mattress as I writhe against his face.

And then my boyfriend's face appears in front of mine. He kisses me deep as another man makes me come, and he's moaning with approval. He's moaning with approval at another man getting me off.

So. Fucking. Hot.

I can't imagine the sheer volume of people who'd sell their very soul to be in my position. It's pure bliss, my back arching as I ride on a bed that really is cloud nine.

Heath peppers me with a path of kisses up my body when I'm in the aftermath of coming, stopping for a suck on one of my tits before he joins Josh.

We share kisses, all three of us a mass of tongues and tastes. Spit and sweat, and the wetness of my pussy still lingering in their mouths.

My hands snake down to find two straining cocks, ready to blow. Two barbelled ladders, veined and scorching.

"My turn for a taste of cum," I say. "Please. Give it to me. Both at once."

I open my mouth wide, and flutter my lashes, grateful beyond belief when the pair of them shuffle up to grant my request.

They aren't so polite with taking turns when it comes to using my mouth, both of them thrusting and driving until I'm hamster cheeked to the max. I love it this way, my head bobbing like the slut I am.

"Take what you asked for, baby. No wasting," Josh says, and his first jet hits the back of my throat. Heath follows suit with a groan, both of them spurting in sync as they come for me. Oh yes, two thick loads of cum filling my mouth as my lips strain around their cock heads...

Luckily, I'm pro enough to handle it. I don't spill a single drop. I swallow it down and smack my lips like a good girl.

What a great start to the holiday.

Both guys collapse at my side when they're done, all three of us grinning up at the ceiling as we soak in the aftermath on Heath's incredible bed.

Welcome to Paradise indeed.

I could happily take an afternoon nap between these two gorgeous men after that tasty escapade, but Heath rolls away from us, off the bed, and goes to the nearest bedside table.

Josh and I prop ourselves up, curious as he pulls out some paperwork from the top drawer.

At least that's what it looks like until he arrives back on the bed and sets the bundle down in front of us.

Envelopes.

Seven envelopes to be precise – with a day written on each one. Starting today.

Sunday.

"And here we have the surprises," Heath says. "Proposals, just like any other client. One for each day of the holiday. And each with a proposal fee that accompanies it."

Heath's proposals are normally so vague when he sends them through via the Agency that they have barely anything written in them. Just a *see you both soon.*

"I've been revisiting the *Naughty List* on the Agency website," he says. "I was missing you, so thought I'd fawn over your profiles, and fell down the rabbit hole of examining your services on offer. I thought I'd have a little playtime exploring them. Variety is the spice of life, after all."

"Proposals?!" I ask. "What, like *actual* proposals?"

"Very detailed fantasies for you to perform, yes," Heath says. "And a proposal fee for each one. Only these fees aren't cash, they are rewards. Treats."

I look at Josh and his eyes are sparkling. His smirk says it all, intrigued, just like I am. The whole idea sounds hot as hell. There are a lot of services on offer on both of our profiles. We are known as *hardcorers* for a reason, and our Naughty List of services get longer and longer by the day.

"So, how about it?" Heath says. "A week's worth of proposals, for a week's worth of treats. Is that acceptable?"

Both Josh and I laugh.

"Treats?" Josh says. "For fulfilling your wildest fantasies? As if we'd need them."

"No treats necessary," I say. "Seriously, Heath. Being in this place with you is a treat enough for seven hundred proposals, not seven."

Heath laughs along with us.

"We'll see if you're still saying that once you've read them. Just one at a time, though. And no sneak peeks or clues."

He pulls us both in for another kiss, and I know one thing. Those proposals would need to be seriously fucking hardcore to need any kind of treat for performing them.

Still, looking at the glint in Heath's eyes when he pulls away from us… I have an inkling they might be.

four

Heath's luxury sun loungers are amazing, set up next to the pool. I'm bathing in the golden sunlight, feeling myself unwind, and I'm realising that I really need this break. But more importantly, so does my boyfriend.

He's on the lounger next to Heath and the both of them are laughing as they recount the first time Josh showed up at Heath's and Josh discovered the identity of User 1543. I've heard the story before, but it always makes me grin.

Apparently, Josh nearly fainted. For real. He had to brace himself against the wall when Heath opened the door. He describes the shock that came over him, and Heath laughs as he recounts how he stepped forward in horror to take Josh by the arm and bundle him inside – suspecting he might need to be calling paramedics, not getting his ass fucked by a male hooker.

"I spend three hours in makeup to be a convincing vampire on the screen, Josh, and you put the makeup team to shame. You were paler than me in three seconds flat."

"Yeah, hardly a surprise, was it? I was expecting a horny weirdo inside the Tim Burton style home, no problem. But the lead star of Nighttime Whispers, paying for an ass fuck. Not quite what I'd figured would be happening. Plus, I was a relative newbie. Not primed for the shocks of the unexpected."

Heath was one of Josh's first clients.

His favourite clients.

I can't imagine that will ever change.

"Will you answer a few questions?" Heath asks my stunning shirtless boyfriend. "Since you're on *vacation* as well as working, how about letting the guard down a bit? I'm curious."

"Curious?"

"Yes." Heath pauses to take a swig of his beer. "Considering how much of an impact running into a TV star on a proposal had for you back then, have you had any similar encounters along the way? Or worse? Have you ever been so bowlegged you collapsed on someone's porch?"

Josh stares up at the sky through his sunglasses, with a smirk on his face.

"Are you fishing for info, Heath? Celebrities you mean?"

"Celebrities, maybe, yes. You could term it that."

"Want to know if I'm fucking any of your co-stars? Is that it?"

Josh is brushing it off, but Heath is serious. I watch him watching Josh, his attention unwavering.

"Not my co-stars. Just… people. Others in the limelight."

Josh beams a cracker of a smile.

"Hell, yeah. My repertoire is a mile long. The list of A-listers on my roster should have me seated at the Brit Awards."

Heath believes him for a second, I see the way he tenses, and Josh laughs.

"You think I'm serious, don't you? Wow. I'm flattered." He pretends to zip his lips up. "I may have come across some celebrities on my roster, literally, but I haven't entered the realms of a Hollywood playboy yet. And even if I had, I wouldn't spill. Confidential, remember? Just like I wouldn't spill to anyone else about you. Not ever." He tips his head towards me. "I didn't even tell Ells. And she's a mega fan."

"Stop it, Josh," I say. "Heath has already heard how many times I've binge watched the first six series. You don't need to keep rubbing it in. I was probably paler than you when I first met him."

My boyfriend props himself up on the lounger and takes off his sunglasses, looking at Heath.

"Wait a second. Is this a tester, more than curiosity? Are you testing me out for confidentiality? Because both Ells and I are fully committed to keeping your identity hidden, Heath. Don't worry."

Heath holds his hands up.

"No, no. Not at all. I trust you both for that. I'm just curious. Interested."

Interested.

I've become much better at reading people now that deep rapport has become part of my career, so I hone in on Heath's smile. His tone. The way his posture shifts.

Hmm.

Interested.

If he's interested in who else manages to knock Josh off his feet as part of his job, the answer to that is nobody. Not that I know of. Not that I *would* know of it, to be fair, since Josh is the master of keeping things under wraps.

Which makes me curious myself…

"Do you actually have other celebrities on your client list?" I ask.

"What?"

"I'm curious, too. You've been in the business a lot longer than me, do you have a whole list of celebs that fill your calendar, or just Heath?"

"What is this, trading cards?" he asks. "You tell me. Do you have any celebrities on your calendar?"

"No. Not besides Heath."

Heath holds up his beer. "I am the one and only."

"Go on," I say to Josh. "Tell us. You're only fuelling the curiosity."

Josh lies back down and folds his arms behind his head.

"Like I said, my lips are sealed. Always."

"You haven't had enough beer yet," Heath laughs. "I'll ask you again when your lips are looser."

"You can try."

"So will I," I chirp in. "I'll try, too."

"Bring it on." I love Josh's sharp confidence. "My lips may get loose, but my mouth never spills."

His respect for his clients' secrecy is admirable, because I know he won't be blabbing. No matter how hard we push him.

Since I started at the Agency, I've spent a fair amount of time contemplating how complicated things can get when it comes to clients. The commonly known *morning after syndrome* – where reality becomes blurred and entertainers get caught up in the proposals so bad that they don't want to leave – is a real thing. It screws some people up, and so do some of the other aspects.

Relationships, with people outside of the business. A lot of people can't handle being in love with a whore and waving them off to a nighttime gig with a *see you later*. Hence, a lot of entertainers end up with other entertainers, and even that has its challenges – a lot of which are the same. Jealousy. Fear. Insecurity. Knowing your partner is out fucking other people at the same time you are, or when you're not. When you're holed up watching TV in your PJs and they're getting it on with three people at once.

I've thought and talked about the dynamics of being an *entertainer* ever since I became one, but as for the dynamic for clients. What it means to be a client... the challenges associated with that... I've never really given it that much thought.

Now that's *interesting*.

Heath has two paid entertainers sharing his private villa right now, one of which he's known and shared a sex life with for years – albeit a paid one. He adores Josh, that much is clear, and there's no doubt in my mind that he's getting pretty fond of me, too. So, how does that work for him?

He said he missed us. Enough that he was browsing our online profiles and checking out our *services*. Was he doing that because he was in a drought? Does he fuck us around fucking other people? Does he fuck other people at all? I know he's not in a relationship, but still. It could still be casual.

Maybe he fucks other whores around our calendar bookings. Maybe he fucks other entertainers. People we know.

The thought of that hits me in the gut, unexpectedly. Bizarre. Because who cares if he does? He could be fucking five other entertainers a week, and why would it matter? Does it matter? It shouldn't. Not to me.

"What are you thinking, Ells?" Josh asks.

"Sorry, what?"

He mimics the lip thing I do when I'm chewing over thoughts.

"Oh, um. Nothing."

"Are you running through a list of celebrities in your head now, wondering if I've screwed them?"

Both guys are staring at me, and I'm a shit liar. Really shit.

"Damnit, Josh. You've got me nailed. I'm going to write a list out later, and quiz you one by one, see if you have any tells I can spot."

"I'm a poker face expert," Josh says. "But you're not."

"No?"

"No. You're looking at Heath. It's him you were thinking about, not me."

He's right. I flash my attention back to Josh in a heartbeat, because I didn't know.

I thought I was developing the ability to read people, but Josh is way up above me, on pretty much everything. I don't want to get into my thoughts on psychology and relationships or morning after syndrome, or any of it, because I'm good when it comes to client confidentiality, but not when it comes to my own.

I get up from the lounger and take off my sunglasses.

"Actually, if you must know, I was thinking about how great Heath's pool looks." I blow him a kiss. "Time for a dip."

"Copout," Josh says, but I'm already dashing across the patio, ready to divebomb.

What a beautiful splash, and what a beautiful pool. I do a few lengths, breaststroke, enjoying the ambience, but I can't get the questions from my mind.

Are we the only people Heath has sex with? Really?

Why do I even hope so?

We've spent many evenings with Heath in London, becoming so comfortable in his mini gothic manor, but here in France it already feels different. More at home than his home, if that is even possible.

And this is just the start.

Seven nights in bed together, seven days at his side. Seven days in his life. Around him. Living with him. *Loving* him.

I'm going to have to be pretty fucking careful, and I know it. Seeing how happy Josh is in his presence only makes the threat more real.

Morning after syndrome might take on a whole new level of serious, and it might be contagious. Taking out Josh as well as me.

I'm staring out over the edge of the infinity pool at the crashing waves on the beach when someone swims up behind me. I have no idea which one of the two guys it is until they appear at my side. Heath. His long, wet hair splaying in the water.

"Josh has gone to grab more beers."

"Cool."

"You're a good swimmer. I enjoyed watching."

"Bah, sure. I was a crappy swimmer at school, and Dad says I do a poodle paddle."

"Poodle paddle or not, it was stunning." Heath's *eyes* are the things that are stunning. Icy blue. The way he looks at me as he talks. "Are you finding this strange, Ella, being here? Are you comfortable?"

I raise my eyebrows.

"Comfortable?! I'm ecstatic, honestly. It's out of this world."

"Out of the regular world, for sure, which is why I'm checking in on you." He gazes out at the sea. "It must be different, such a long proposal, with so much history between me and Josh. If that makes you feel strange, or it crosses any lines, please say so. I'll understand if you want to leave."

I let out a gentle sigh as I admire the horizon.

"Quite the opposite, actually." I lean against him. "You should be more worried about us wanting to stay than wanting to leave. You might need to turf us out before we take up residence."

"Touche." He wraps a strong arm around me. Heath Mason wrapping an arm around me in his swimming pool. Another round of butterflies. "Good job I have season seven of Nighttime coming up, eh? Otherwise we might all want to take up residence for a while, and not just for the proposals."

I love the dirty grin he shoots me.

"I'm so looking forward to proposal number one," he says.

"So am I. When do we get it?"

"Soon, curva. Don't you worry."

He swims off when Josh returns with the beers, but I stay awhile, splashing around in the water while they yap away on the sun loungers. I watch their body language. The way they are so at ease. The way they inch closer and closer as they laugh. Heath's lounger is in danger of tipping, he's leaning so far over the edge.

It's not jealousy, or rage, or concern that washes over me when he finally reaches out and pulls my boyfriend towards him. They kiss so naturally that it's nothing short of beautiful – Josh kissing our client like it's one of the most regular things in the world. *And one of the most wonderful.*

I don't care what proposal number one entails, so long as it entails anything, and real fucking soon.

The guys must be feeling it too, since the moment the kiss is broken Heath raises a hand to beckon me over.

"How about some dinner, Ella?"

"Sure thing. Thanks."

There are a few things I'd much prefer to be eating, but dinner will have to come first.

I can feel the static in the air amidst the chatter and laughter as the three of us prep a chicken and potato salad together. We eat it on one of the terraces, with the sun on the decline in an awesome sunset. Our beer drinking slows down, but the tension ramps up – the inevitable is hanging between us.

Proposal number one.

That's what I want for dessert tonight, not the meringue Heath kindly offers to make us.

"Meringue can wait for me, thanks, it's an envelope I'm after," Josh says. "Time is ticking, and my balls are tingling."

"And you, Ella?" Heath asks as he gathers up our plates from the terrace table. "Meringue for you? Or are you too tingly yourself?"

"Far too tingly for meringue, kind sir. Envelopes all the way, please."

I take our empty beers and Josh takes the bottles of sauces, following Heath back into the villa and through to the kitchen. I load the dishwasher along with Josh as Heath disappears to the bedroom, and my heart catches in my throat when I see the envelope in his hand on his return.

Josh gives me the honours, gesturing that Heath gives it to me for opening, and I flip it over in my hands, my heart racing.

Here it is. The first mystery about to be revealed.
Proposal number one.
I can't wait to get started.

five

SUNDAY

This may be a week of vacation pleasure, but let's not forget. I am the client here, and my wishes are your command. Proposal one is here to reinforce that.
Tonight, I am the one in charge. I will be the puppet master, and the pair of you will be my toys.
The question is... who is going to be my favourite? Who is going to be the best performing puppet at the show?
I want your gorgeous 'curva' asses. Spread, needy and hungry for action.
Let's see how rough you can take it. How deep you can take it. And how fucking whorish you can be while you're taking it.
No holds barred, guys. Holes open wide.
Mine as well as yours.
Give me all you've got, and I'll return the favour when I'm done with you.

Proposal duration – Until I find the depths and dig even deeper.
Reward – A lovely massage and pamper day, to aid in your recovery.

*H*eath is smiling as I read the words aloud, but it isn't his beaming grin from the terrace earlier. His gaze is sultry, dirty… determined. He means business, and so he should. We are indeed the *curvas*, and he is indeed the client.

"Puppet master, hey?" Josh asks him, then runs his tongue over his bottom lip. "What are you going to do? Impale us on your fists and get us to sing Bohemian Rhapsody?"

Heath raises an eyebrow. "Who knows what you'll be singing by the time I'm finished with you. Stop it with the backchat. You're giving me ideas."

Josh leans against the kitchen counter, folding his arms with his usual filthy boy smirk, and I look between him and Heath, sensing the tension. It sizzles.

"You've had plenty of ideas already," Josh says. "It's all played out in your filthy mind. I know you, Heath. Remember that."

Heath steps towards him, closing the distance. "And I know *you*. Remember that." He runs a thumb over Josh's cheek. "I know you'd happily be my fist puppet and sing whatever fucking tune I wanted."

Josh's eyes are so fierce on Heath's.

"If it's in the proposal, sure. I never let my clients down." He looks towards me. "And neither does Ella, do you, baby?"

I shake my head.

"Never. No way. I'll be singing along to the same tune all night long."

Josh grins. "You wouldn't want to be singing Bohemian Rhapsody though, would you?"

He starts humming the theme tune to Nighttime Whispers. Cheeky bastard.

I imagine bouncing on Heath's fist, trying to crescendo the song lyrics with Josh beside me, both of us trying to ride in sync. It's so darkly fucked up I laugh out loud, but at the same time, it gives me tingles. Whatever the hell had been written in Heath's proposal would have made me horny. And that's the thing... as crazy as it might sound, I'm coming to expect crazy. To embrace crazy. To ride the crazy, wherever it takes me. Especially where an idol like Heath is concerned.

I don't think we'll truly be singing tunes tonight, but as for being fist puppets? That seems right up Heath's street. I wouldn't put it past him on the stretch-play front, and I wouldn't want to. And from the way he's staring at Josh, I'd say the idea is pretty solid in his mind.

"Serious now, curva," Heath says. "You won't be laughing when you're begging your *master* on the floor. The proposal starts now."

Shit. Ok. I haven't had much time to prepare. I'm blustering around, thinking maybe I should get dressed up like a decent gothic curva, but Josh never blusters when he's on the spot. He's cool as a cucumber.

I start as he takes hold of Heath's chin. His movement snake-like, he's so fucking quick.

"The question is, how loud are you gonna sing when it's your turn?" Josh asks our vampire lord. "You'll take it right back when you're done with us."

Heath raises his eyebrows. "Dirty talk like that is only going to make me push you harder."

"Good. I want you to push it all the fucking way. Treat me like a dirty puppet, and it'll be coming right back at you."

"I know that. I wrote the fucking proposal."

The tension is ramping. The dynamic between them makes me heady, it's so palpable.

I can't help but drop the proposal envelope when my boyfriend lands his lips on our client's. It slips from my hand and goes sailing to the floor, because I'm so mesmerised by the scene unfolding. Josh and Heath's ferocity takes me aback as they kiss and groan – Josh spinning to slam Heath into the counter. Josh can switch both ways, but with Heath he loves to lead. He loves to drive and push, and stretch. It will be a gorgeous strain for him to accept Heath as the master on night one.

Heath shoves Josh away and snaps his fingers before he points at the floor.

"Strip and serve," Heath says to my boyfriend, then beckons me forward with a wave of his hand. "You too, Ella. I want both of you naked, right now. On your knees. Time to get this filthy puppet show underway."

His voice sounds like the Count's on Nighttime Whispers – the deep, dark tone he uses when he's asserting control. My body responds before my brain does, ditching the bikini I'm still wearing from the terrace without a second thought. I'm over to him in seconds, dropping to my knees in time with Josh once he's stripped from his t-shirt and shorts. I cast a glance at Josh's hard cock, already impressive and veiny. I'm so tempted to reach over and grip the gorgeous barbelled shaft, but Heath clears his throat, drawing my attention straight back up to our *master.*

His smile is sly. He leans back against the worktop, still clothed in his own t-shirt and shorts.

"Such beautiful creatures," he says. "So eager to do my bidding."

He points at the floor.

"Lower."

"Lower?" I ask.

"Yes. Lower. Pray at my fucking feet like good sluts. Balasana!"

I've been practising yoga with Josh as part of his workouts back in London. The flexibility helps no end in our line of work. Still, I haven't used it like this before.

Balasana. The child position.

I can feel the prickly heat from Josh, wanting to fight back and haul Heath to the floor along with us, but he doesn't do it. He does as he's told, lowering his torso, so his forehead is resting on the floor. It looks like a plea for mercy when he stretches out his arms in front of him.

The aircon works like a dream in this place, so I know the glorious marble floor tiles are going to be cold against my skin. I give Heath a moan and graze my nipples against the chill first, arching myself into the cobra position to display my tits before heeding his command for balasana, my forehead touching the floor.

I hear Heath walking back and forth, his bare feet just shy of our outstretched fingers as he makes us wait for our next instruction.

"Forward, come towards me," he says, and I feel so awkward as I shuffle along, maintaining the pose. "Further. Faster. Now."

The floor is brutal against my knees, my tits dragging.

"Stop," he says.

I stop moving and risk a glance at Josh to find him still in position along with me. We're lined up well, neck and neck, with an ocean of space around us. My ears are on hyper alert as Heath walks around us, full circle. I hear every footstep – slow and steady. He does three laps before he comes to a halt at the rear.

"How does it feel to be back in service?" he asks. "Subject to whatever fantasy I desire?"

I'm smiling at the floor as I answer.

"It feels amazing, *sir*."

Heath's laugh is dry. "Ah, yes. My sweet Ella. Always so many *amazings* from your pretty mouth. How about you, Joshua? How does it feel for you, you dirty curva?"

"Cold. This floor is freezing." He pauses. "But hot. You're always a fucking scorcher, Heath, whatever you do."

"Hands back now," Heath says. "Spread your asses for me. Let's get the heat ramped up."

My forehead is still pressed tight to the floor as I reach back and spread my ass cheeks. I shuffle my legs wider, so Heath can see my pussy too, panting at what is to come. Am I really going to be a puppet for him? Seriously? What's he going to do? I hear a pop of something opening... a bottle maybe, and I lurch forward as something lands on me from above. A drizzle of liquid, all over my back, before it runs like a river down my butt crack.

"Olive oil," Heath says, and I guess he must be doing the same to Josh when the drizzle stops. "Such a good lube."

We were enjoying olive oil on our salad earlier, I didn't think I'd be enjoying the sensation of it dribbling over my asshole just a few hours later.

I hear Heath stripping from his clothes, and damn, how I wish I could get a sight. I'm still spreading my ass for him as he drops to his knees behind us.

"Puppet holes." His laugh is pure filth. "Oh, fuck, how I've missed my beautiful playthings."

His fingers run up and down the oily river of my ass crack before he slides two inside. I gasp, adoring the wet plunge.

"I was only playing on words about being the puppet master, but you've given me ideas, Josh. You have yourself to blame." He pauses. "Or thank."

"Pretty certain it will be a thanks," Josh says before he grunts.

I want to look back and see what Heath is doing to him, but I'd topple over if I tried.

"Your ideas will only fuel mine," Josh says. "Practice what you preach, and reap what you sow."

"Get your asses higher," Heath tells us. "Up in the air, spread those cheeks for me."

I gather myself with another shuffle, my head turned to the side as I offer myself to Heath. Josh is mirroring me, and my eyes lock on his as I feel something sliding into my butt. Metal. And then a glug. Jesus. I feel a slosh of something slopping its way inside me. Oh my God. Heath has poured olive oil straight inside my asshole. It feels slimy, but weirdly fucking amazing.

"Your turn now, darling," Heath says, and my stare is locked on Josh's perfect face as he closes his eyes, clearly savouring the sensation as Heath does the same to him.

"It was a tough call, Ella," our client says as he slips two fingers back inside my gloopy ass. "I've been desperate for your cunt, truly, but I'm going to be pulling the same puppet strings for both of you. It's only fair."

I barely groan when Heath pushes three fingers into my ass instead of two, I'm so slick and lubed. I love anal, and my oily ass is craving an invasion. I want to be Heath's fucking puppet. I want him to use my ass like a fucking toy. I grip his three fingers as tightly as I can, but the oil makes gripping anything practically impossible.

My headspace switches like a lightning strike when Heath shoves in four at once, and I'm Holly the whore on Heath's kitchen floor. I'm murmuring, *begging*, because I need more.

"Who is going to top the leaderboard tonight?" he asks. "Who is the most hardcore entertainer for proposal number one?"

Heath is playing with fire, stoking flames of competition, and he knows it. I always want to top the charts and be the best entertainer every chance I get. I strive for the greatest hardcorer status with every single proposal I attend. And so does Josh…

"When it comes to ass play, you know who'll be the winner," Josh says to Heath, but he's looking at me with a smirk. "Ella's ass is not such an easy target as mine. She's less experienced."

Josh has the mischievous glint in his eyes that gives me butterflies. He's goading me.

"I may be less experienced, but if you want a filthy puppet, I'll give you a filthy puppet," I say, and push back against Heath's fingers. "Why don't you try me for size?"

Heath's laugh is gentle but deadly.

"Be careful, Ella. This is only day one, remember? You have a full week of proposals yet to perform."

His words only drive me on. My clit sparks, wanting to serve and succeed.

"Make me a puppet, Heath." I bounce my ass against his squelching fingers. "Whatever you do to Josh, do to me. I'm not coming second."

"You can compete, if you really want to. Sing your songs. Use your words. Tell me how desperate you are to have my fist in your oily fucking holes."

Josh and I are both a flurry of grunts, groans and fucking whimpers as we go for it, looking at each other all the while we beg Heath to plug his fist in deep. I splay my ass cheeks as wide as I possibly can, cursing under my breath as he twists his knuckles deep to loosen me.

This is fucking crazy.

Competing with my boyfriend to take Heath's fist deepest and hardest, lubed up with olive oil on a kitchen floor.

I see the grimace on Josh's face when he bucks up against Heath's fist, and he's outdone me. I hear the squelch as Heath's hand sinks all the way in. Fuck it. I'm still at the knuckles. Heath is still twisting and loosening me, since I'm not ready to take him. My ass is still protesting, burning despite the olive oil, but I'm out of my head with the need to keep up. I want to feel the pop of force as my ass accepts him.

"Please!" I say. "Heath, please, just do it."

"Very well," he says.

It's a white heat that has me biting off a yelp when Heath plunges in in one. I breathe hard, trying to stay relaxed around the hand inside me, but Heath is already fist-fucking Josh with a passion. I can hear the beautiful slick rhythm as he pulls his fist in and out, and Josh is grinning, bucking… giving it *more, more, more* as he takes it like a pro.

I give up on splaying my ass cheeks and brace myself on the floor instead, and I may be a cheater on all fours, but it puts me back in the game. It's *me* bucking now, taking Heath's hand in and out of me like a dirty little slut.

"Unfair advantage," Josh says, and mirrors me – going doggy position to buck just as fast.

"Bastard," I laugh. "You're so competitive, you know that?"

"Says you. Queen of the leaderboard."

Josh reaches out to pull me closer, and I inch over to him, our sides pressed together as our client treats us like a pair of gloves. Josh's breaths are in my face, his eyes just inches from mine, and the competition eases. I want to kiss him so fucking bad, but he beats me to it, managing to land his lips on mine before I get the chance.

Heath clears his throat.

"I'm buried wrist deep in your asses like a Punch and fucking Judy show, and you two are making out like teenagers. Remember who's in charge here."

He slams us particularly hard… once, twice, three times, and then he pulls out – my ass feeling like it's belching open before he plunges back in again. A ravaged fucking cave. I can't make out with Josh under this kind of barrage. There is nothing but the thumping invasion of Heath's fist as he punches his way in deeper.

"Oh the fucking view," Heath says. "Stunning."

I look back at him over my shoulder, and it's an *oh the fucking view* for myself at the sight of Heath's smile. His hair is hanging free as he punch fucks us, his eyes a dirty delight as he plunges inside.

"How about we call Ella the winner?" Josh says. "Please, Heath. Share the bounty. I want to see your fist in Ella's ass. I want to see how deep she's fucking taking it."

My eyes are still on Heath as he smirks at my boyfriend.

"Since you asked so nicely, how could I refuse? Here, come and assist me."

I get a flutter of panic as Heath pulls out of Josh's ass and sets him free, because I'm already taking so much it's insane.

Both men are positioned behind me, and my mind whirs – my dirty curva side battling with rationale.

"That's really fucking impressive," Josh says. "Here, pull out, just a bit… like that. Fuck, yes."

I know I'm gaping, with the two of them staring inside me. I know what a display of pure messy filth it must look like, to see my oily open ass after such a pounding.

"You've been so good, baby," Josh tells me, and hooks his hand around my thigh to reach my pussy. My clit sparks like an electric shock when his fingers land, and he circles slowly, like a tease. "Take our client's fist nice and deep again now. Give him the performance of the night."

Heath's hand sinks back in, and the sensations are all mashed up. Sparks of pleasure mixed with the tender burnout of pain. It aches so bad but feels so good.

"More oil," Heath says, and I feel a fresh glug sinking into me. It sounds so wet when Heath starts back up with the invasion, and he's not fast this time. He's slow. Slow and fucking deep.

Deeper than he was before…

So deep that I can feel the oil oozing out of me and dribbling over my pussy.

I cry out when he keeps burying, scooping his hand this way and that, and Josh speeds his fingers on my oily clit.

"It's ok, baby, focus on me and be a good puppet for Heath. He's so far in, Ella. It's fucking beautiful."

I cry out again as the pressure resumes, Heath's hand still claiming more.

"Make her come," Heath says. "Make the sweet curva come for me, Josh. I want her to come while I'm all the way in."

Josh is a wizard with my clit, strumming with so much precision I'm gasping in seconds, but I let out another cry as Heath eases in just a little bit more and it feels like he's inside my belly.

I'm a fucking hand puppet. A dirty, used, wrecked hand puppet, with a fist so deep it could be in my fucking guts – and it's gross, and invasive, and slimy, and aches along with the burn, but it still turns me on. In fact, it turns me on more than ever.

"Do you trust me, baby?" Josh asks, and I nod with a crazy smile.

A question like that only means one thing.

It means more.

"Stay nice and relaxed, ok… just relax…"

Oh my fucking God, I feel his other hand slipping between my thighs from behind. He's still strumming my clit, and Heath is still buried when two of Josh's fingers seek out my slippery cunt.

"Trust me," Josh says, and his two fingers spear my pussy, angled against Heath's hand. Such a thin wall, and so sensitive.

"I can't…" I pant. "I can't…"

But I'm wrong. Josh's fingers curl inside me, battling for space, and his strumming of my clit sends me over the edge. I'm a grunting whore when I come for the pair of them, squirting with such high pressure that it must look like I'm pissing all over the floor. I daren't move, so I just brace myself, riding the waves. I'm so full. So crazy fucking full, that I'm scared to rock, or writhe, or anything. I just let the men play my body like a fucked up melody of filth.

I guess you could call that singing. Just not with vocals.

Heath is very gentle as he unplugs his fist from me. I collapse onto the floor in the aftermath, rolling onto my back in the oil slick.

I shake my head as I stare up at both of them, still in disbelief that the puppet show made it that far.

"That was crazy."

"Crazy hot," Heath says, and holds up his dirty slick hand. I can see the band of oil on his wrist. No joke he was buried deep. "Well done, curva. That was truly delightful."

Heath is grinning down at me when Josh's smile turns. I'm practically a mind reader when it comes to my boyfriend now. The change in his energy gives me a lurch so strong I feel nauseous.

He's gunning for the man who just puppet fisted us. He's already stretching his fingers, ready for action.

"And you, Josh," Heath says, and flicks his attention back to my boyfriend.

That's when he clocks it, too. The change in chemistry. The vicious need in Josh's eyes.

"Practice what you preach, and reap what you sow, remember?" Josh licks his lips. "Time for you to get your fucking ass in the air now, Heath. You're gonna need a whole load of olive oil after that show."

Josh is so rough as he tangles his fist in Heath's hair and shunts him forward onto all fours beside me. I scuffle out of the way, my eyes wide as my boyfriend reaches for the half empty bottle of oil and pops the top off.

Josh's cock is straining, proud. Veined and dark and ready to blow.

"Spread your fucking ass," he orders Heath. "You can be a sweet *curva* now."

Heath does as he's told, breaths shallow. I catch sight of his cock, and he's as hard as Josh is – the puppet master desperate for a puppet master of his own. And he's going to get one.

I back myself up so I can watch Josh at work. Heath's dirty fingers are splaying his own cheeks, his ass clenching in preparation for what's to come. A glorious target.

Josh doesn't bother with slicking up Heath's crack, just pushes the pourer of the olive oil bottle straight in and empties the whole fucking lot of it – a tank of lube sinking straight into Heath's ass.

Heath groans as Josh gets to work, and my entire body tingles as I watch my boyfriend take control.

"There's no competition for you, *curva*, so you're just going to have to take what you're given. But that's what you want, isn't it? To take what you're fucking given?"

My vampire hero nods, his groans notching up as Josh plugs straight in to the knuckles.

"Yes. I want to take what I'm fucking given. So give it to me. Do it, Josh. Fist my dirty fucking ass like I fisted your girlfriend's."

I've seen things get rough between Josh and Heath before. I've seen both of their asses take each other's fists and accept one hell of a pounding, but this is different. Josh is plunging our client like he's delving for treasure, loosening Heath to take a clenched fist before sliding in, fingers first.

Deep.

Really fucking deep.

As deep as Heath can take it…

And then more.

Just like Heath did with me.

It's absolutely stunning to see the fire in Josh's eyes as he puts Heath through the same beautiful torture he inflicted on me, and music to my ears to hear the way Heath grunts as he struggles to take it.

Josh's eyes are still scorching hot when he looks at me.

"Be a good curva for Heath now, and milk his needy cock, will you? I want him to come while I'm at my deepest."

The request lights up my soul.

"My pleasure."

And it is my pleasure.

Reaching underneath Heath to grip his barbelled shaft is a dream come true. And two hands mean double the dream. I have a free one at my disposal to grip Josh's cock at the same time, milking them both in tandem.

Damn, I'm good at it.

They come practically in sync – Josh's fist buried deep in Heath's perfect ass when the first jet of cum blows, and he takes advantage of it. One tiny shunt forward that makes Heath curse with a *fuck!*

He groans louder than we did, daring to shunt backwards as he's coming. I jerk his cock faster, milking every drop. Kudos to him, he's really fucking incredible, and I'm a lucky girl to get the chance to watch him. He's hot enough to set the villa on fire.

There is one clear winner of the puppet show when the two guys compare filthy hands in the aftermath. I may have taken a decent chunk of Heath's wrist inside me, but the ring of oil on Josh's forearm says it all. It's at least three inches higher.

Heath may have been the puppet master, but he's been the greatest puppet of all three of us tonight.

He should be getting the pamper and recovery reward tomorrow, not us.

But still, I'll take it gladly.

six

A night of sleep in Heath's cloud bed could never be topped. I wake up to bright sunlight streaming in through the windows. It's a heaven of slumber.

So is the heaven of rolling over and seeing the pair of them still deep in dreamland. Josh facing me, with Heath's arm wrapped around his waist from behind.

I rise just a touch on my pillows so I can see our beautiful client, snoozing softly with his gorgeous dark hair fanned out. He's a masterpiece. And if I wasn't with Josh – the man my heart belongs to without question – I'd most certainly want to be with him.

Morning after syndrome is going to hit like a bitch when we touch back down to life in London. Thank fuck it's only day two of seven.

Josh wakes first, his long lashes fluttering before his eyes open and land on mine. He reaches out and pulls me closer, and the feeling of flesh on flesh is so good I could stay here all day. It's enough of a pamper day already without our proposal *fee* from last night.

Heath stirs, rolling away enough to stretch his arms up over his head. I look at his hands, clenching my ass at the memory of how deep he plugged me last night. I'm still burning, but that doesn't matter. I'd take it all over again.

Just as well, since I probably will.

"Morning, *curvas*," Heath says. "Did you sleep well?"

"Well would be an understatement," I say. "It was amazing."

He props himself up on an elbow. "How about you, Joshua?"

"As if you need to ask."

He pulls Heath in for a kiss on the lips like it's the most natural thing in the world, which gives me tingles. This isn't roleplay. It isn't characterisation, or being *in service*, or proposal territory, and it's not a prelude to another bout of horny action, either.

It's affection.

It's…

No. I can't go there. Not even to ponder.

Heath is User 1543, and this is a job. For Josh as well as me.

"Ready for pamper day?" Heath asks, and Josh wrestles him over, so he's on top of both of us. A sleepy pile up.

"Fuck pamper day," Josh says, guiding Heath's face to mine.

It's a full-on tangle of a kiss when Heath's lips land, and I squirm instinctively, my horny pussy ready for a round of cock. But Heath pulls away.

"You deserve your *fee*," he says. "No fees, no proposals."

I watch him as he rises from the bed, his perfect ass a sight to behold. I want to see Josh's cock buried in him. I want, I want, I want… everything.

"Come on," Heath says. "Shift your cute butts. Pamper day starts right now."

"No choice, have we?" Josh says with a smirk. "No way we're losing out on proposal number two." He slaps Heath's ass as he gets out of bed to join him. "You're a darling, you know that? Pampering us so generously when we are the ones here to pamper you."

Josh isn't wrong.

A delivery of fresh fruit and pastries arrives once the three of us are done in the bathroom. We sit in robes on the terrace, munching down croissants and fruit salad while sipping on top end espresso, and Heath looks so happy as he eats with us.

My question comes without even thinking.

"Who are you usually here with?"

I shouldn't ask questions so pointed. He's a client and it's confidentiality at all costs. But that's the thing. I've a been a fan of Heath Mason for years, but even Google has virtually nothing to say about his personal life. Believe me, I've been digging.

It's always speculation about partners in the news stories – hot co-stars on the red carpet, but nothing concrete. Nothing real. Not for all of the years I've been fangirling, anyway.

"Sorry, that's none of my business," I add, but Heath doesn't flinch.

"Nobody comes here with me. You could say I'm quite the loner. *Introverted.*"

I get a pang at that. I don't know why. Just the idea of Heath being a loner, when he could be surrounded by so many people. He's an icon for millions.

"I do have a brother," he says. "But he has a family up in Nottingham. We meet up occasionally, but we don't really click as personalities." He takes a sip of his coffee. "Finlay is about as opposite from me as it gets. Not goth and certainly not bi."

Fuck it. I keep the questions rolling.

"What about your parents?"

"They passed away nine years ago."

Oh shit. That was before Nighttime Whispers started. They would never have seen Heath as the Count. I'm sure they would have been so proud.

He must read my face.

"No, they never saw it. They saw me in bit parts, and walk-ons, but I was already orphaned when I landed Whispers. I walked the red carpet alone for series one. Finn and Marlie didn't accept the invitation to join me. They didn't want the spotlight on their family."

I swear I see a flash of sadness in Heath's eyes, and I want to call his brother a wanker, but I've already overstepped the mark far enough.

Josh is casual on the lounger next to me. He doesn't interrupt or join in, and I wonder how much he already knows about Heath. Far more than me, that's for sure, but how much?

Josh will never tell me. His mouth might as well have a padlock on it when it comes to clients' personal lives. Even Heath's.

"Nighttime Whispers went to my head for a while," Heath says. "Everyone wanted a piece of me once I hit the spotlight, and I bought into the bullshit. I was surrounded by *friends*, partying from dusk until dawn. *Friends* who wanted my cock as well as my company. And plenty more besides."

"Plenty more? Wow. As if your cock and company wouldn't be enough. What more could they possibly want from you?" I giggle, and take another slice of melon.

Heath looks at me almost wistfully. His smile is so stunning, it's insane.

"Oh, Ella, how beautiful it is to see such a genuine soul. So sweet. So well meaning."

Something clicks that I haven't felt before around Heath. I've been such a fan for so long, that even here I've been holding him on some kind of celebrity pedestal without even realising it. The man looking at me isn't the Count, or the groomed star of Whispers.

He's just a guy.

A guy with a huge amount of wealth and prestige, yeah, but just a guy.

A loner.

"They wanted a lot more from me than my cock and company," Heath says. "Try adding cash, contacts, celebrity status, leg-ups into the industry. People crying out to be on my arm in front of the cameras, with enough behind the scenes *gossip* to flog it to magazines for a decent payout."

I pause as I take in his words.

I remember how hungry my ex-boyfriend Connor was for fame, chasing 'contacts' at any cost. Prepared to sell out anything for a shot at the limelight – including me.

"I'm sorry," I say.

"There's nothing to be sorry for," Heath replies and gestures around us. "I have a glorious existence. The luxury of being surrounded by luxury, and still being passionate about my career. I don't need the glory of showbusiness to gain meaning from my performance on screen." He pauses. "And I have you. Two incredible people who can indulge my needs and fantasies without ulterior motives."

"No chance we'd sell you out. Not ever," I say. "You can count on that, *Count*."

"I know." He smiles at Josh. "I discovered that about *Weston* a long time ago, and I was blessed to find a likeminded soul in you, *Holly*. I'm glad you are a couple and not just coworkers. You deserve each other."

You deserve love, too. That's what I want to say. He deserves what me and Josh have. Adoration, commitment, trust. A life with someone who wants to share it, through all of the good and bad.

Heath claps his hands, clearly marking the conversation as done and finished.

"Let's get onto the next part of pamper day, shall we? We have a lot of ground to cover before proposal two, and I certainly don't want to be late starting."

"Me neither," Josh says and glugs back the rest of his coffee.

I go along with the pair of them with a smile, though my guts are churning with the need to know more. I want to know Heath's soul. I want to know his history. I want to know everything. I've spent a lot of time with him during proposals, but it's not the same as here. This place feels like a whole other league.

Josh takes my wrist as Heath dashes to the sunroom to open the door.

"Don't push him too hard," Josh whispers, his mouth up against my ear. "He's taken a lot of shit. He needs a vacation, not a therapy week, baby."

"Sure," I say, and Josh plants a kiss on the top of my head.

Whoa, Heath really has set up a pamper room. Two massage tables lined up, with beautiful bouquets of flowers in vases on the windowsill. There's a huge display on the wall at the far end, like a top-notch salon, and he beckons me over with a *tada!* Shelves packed with body lotions and skincare products. Massage oils and lotions, and balms, and so many moisturisers you could open a store. I recognise some of the brands, and these things come with a hefty price tag.

"I have to keep myself in top condition for set," he says.

I pick up one of the bottles. I've seen this one mentioned online – a vanilla and coconut cleanser that the influencers rave about. I open the lid to smell it. The raving isn't unfounded.

"You can be my guest, literally," Heath says. "Empty the whole wall if you want to. Just let me treat you to a session first."

"We can take some of them?" I ask.

"You are welcome to take all of them, curva. I can restock my collection. They usually send them out to me for free." He points to the massage tables. "Up on there, please, both of you. Robes off, nice and relaxed. I'll do your backs first."

I grin at Josh as we take a massage table each, both of us positioning ourselves face down. The padding feels great against my tits.

Heath lights up a scented candle, and puts on some soft music, sounding out ocean waves and wind chimes. It's me he comes to first, laying his hands on my back to slather me in a balm that feels like butter.

His hands are magical, strong and firm as he works his fingers into my flesh. I didn't know he was such a skilled masseur – yet another talent to add to his collection. He unknots knots I didn't even know I had. My shoulders ease, and my back loosens, and when Heath reaches my ass, he kneads me like dough, digging his knuckles into my hips as he works.

"You're so good at this," I say, and he chuckles.

"Maybe I should take it up as a sideline."

"Please don't. I need at least eight hundred seasons of Whispers."

I fight the urge to spread my thighs as he keeps moving down my body. I want his skilled fingers on my pussy as well as the rest of me. *More* than the rest of me. Still, he moves on, down to my feet where he works harder still, grinding his thumbs into the arches.

I'm so chilled out that I could lie here for ever by the time he moves over to Josh. I turn my head so I can watch him, and the concentration on his face is magnificent. His hands work with such instinct. Such precision. Josh moans in pleasure as Heath uses an elbow on a particularly tense knot under his shoulder blade.

Fuck, yes. Right there.

I'm floating in la la land, timeless as Heath pampers my boyfriend. I'm hazy when he finishes up Josh's feet and returns to me with a fresh variety of creams.

"Turn over for me, curva."

Heath gives me a facial of a different kind than I'm used to from my clients. It's usually cum caking my cheeks when I'm around him, not skin cream. Again, he's so good, leaving the moisturiser on as he moves his attention down to my tits. A breast massage, fuck, how good it feels. Too good. My breaths are shallow as he works lotion into my skin, bearing down hard as he palms me, and it's too much. I loll my thighs open, silently begging him to work his magic on my pussy.

"Not yet," he says.

"Please… just a taster."

He brushes a thumb across my slit.

"That's all your getting for now. I'm saving your cunt for proposal two."

"Tease."

"You'll thank me for it later."

Somehow, I doubt that. My body is already screaming out for his cock, as well as his magic fingers.

I'll be tearing the envelope open when he offers it, I'll be so desperate.

I'm not the only one who's desperate. When it's Josh's turn to turn over, his cock is rock solid, but Heath doesn't break and give in to his requests, either.

We must have been in the pamper session for two hours when Heath finishes and beckons us back over to the product shelf. He's so ridiculously generous with the gifts that my arms are loaded with bottles and tubs when we leave. I might even need another suitcase.

Again, it hits me how much a man like Heath deserves the love that Josh and I share, but the thought of him finding someone and having to say goodbye to us… it makes me feel sick.

We sip on champagne, swim lengths, and make small talk for the rest of the afternoon, with a late lunch salad to fill us up before dinner. The tension begins to crackle in the air as the sun goes down – proposal two soon to be in sight. I hope dinner is a quick one so we can get down to it.

"What are we having?" I ask when we get back into the kitchen, and Heath smirks and taps his nose.

"Wouldn't want to spoil the surprise now. Let the envelope do the talking."

"I meant, what are we having for dinner," I say.

"And I meant what I said," he says, "we'll let the envelope do the talking."

He disappears off to the bedroom as both Josh and I watch him, and I turn to my boyfriend with a shrug.

"Any ideas?" I ask, and Josh tips his head from side to side. Again, it's obvious he knows Heath far better than I do when he shoots me a cracking smile.

"I might have a few, yes."

Damnit, I'm so intrigued I want to sprint after Heath and tear the envelope from his fingers.

seven

MONDAY

It was a tough call as to who would be my food table for the evening, but Ella, you will have the honour of being the platter board.
Your tits will make an awestriking set of dinner plates.
You will keep your gorgeous body still and stable at all times, eat only when you are offered food, and serve in whichever way you are required.
No words, please. Tables don't talk!
Be prepared for both very hot and very cold substances. You will be the serving table for all three courses.

Proposal duration - three hours.
Reward - an exclusive preview of the upcoming series of Nighttime Whispers.

I'm buzzing when Heath reads the proposal aloud. I'd happily be a table for five days straight for a preview of even one episode of the new series. People have been hyping it up for months, and the last one finished up on an asshole of a cliffhanger. Will the Count catch and bite Polly Anna or not?!

"I take it that's a yes?" Heath asks as I grab the piece of paper from him, open mouthed.

"Um, let me think about it for a second. YES!"

"See if you're still saying that at the end of three courses."

"I'd stake my soul on it."

"Interesting choice of words."

Josh ruffles my hair. "What a winner for landing the proposal this evening, Ells. The reward of your dreams. Make sure you're not too good at being a table, or we'll ditch the one from the apartment and you can take up the permanent honour."

"Screw that, Josh. I enjoy my pizza nights on the sofa, thank you very much."

Heath points over to the dining table. The one at the far end of the kitchen diner. "It isn't pizza we'll be serving tonight, Ella. It's something more… sensual."

I clap my hands, trying to shove thoughts of Nighttime Whispers to the side. I have other pleasures to be focusing on right now.

"Back or front?"

"On your back, please. Naked and ready. Think of it as a different kind of massage table."

It's easy to get undressed living here with Heath, since I'm wearing virtually nothing day to day. I ditch my robe and dash over to climb up onto the table, positioning myself. This certainly isn't the padded luxury I was lying on in the pamper room earlier, but it's exciting. The table is a solid, light wood with enough space to stretch my arms up over my head and lay my legs flat.

"Who's going to be the chef?" I ask, but Heath steps up with a finger over his lips.

"Tables don't speak, remember."

"Sorry."

"In addition to that, tables don't have eyes." Heath pulls out a black satin blindfold from the pocket of his robe. I raise my head so he can fasten it in position. "Remember, curva, tables stay still. No moving. You'll only get the reward if you pass the challenge."

Apart from the blindfold, Heath doesn't bind me. My limbs are free to move, and my body is able to squirm – which is going to make obeying commands so much harder. In bondage, there is no choice but to stay in position, but this kind of stillness is going to require some effort.

I know Heath is going to push me, but I'm going to succeed. I'll be the best table in the world for even a glimpse at the new NW.

It feels like I'm waiting an age, blindfolded and bare on the top of Heath Mason's table. I can hear the guys talking in the kitchen area – giving me lewd compliments amidst their general chatter. I hear pans and chopping boards being taken out and used, but besides from that there is no clue as to what's on the menu. They could be making anything. Until I smell the onion in the air…

I hear the stirring of a pan. A sauce, maybe? Whatever it is smells delicious, and my stomach rumbles. It seems a long time since I ate last. The wood feels harder under my back, and my body has the instinct to move. To shuffle into a different position. But I don't. I don't break the proposal.

Somehow, even through the chatter and the dinner making, I know the guys will be keeping a close eye on my every movement. Or lack of it. It's horny to be at the mercy of words on a piece of paper, but at the same time I wish I was a part of their duo, joining in on the kitchen action.

My stomach is rumbling hard when footsteps approach. I hear a guy on either side of me, and the clank of metal above.

"This is going to be delicious," Heath says, from my left. "Nice and hot. Soup makes an excellent starter."

And just like that, my rumbling stomach is covered in a thick river of liquid, so hot I hold my breath, because it hurts. The splatter really fucking scorches. I grit my teeth when the torrent dribbles over my tits, bracing myself until it begins to chill, and oh fuck. Oh fuck, fuck, fuck! The pan clanks before another load starts up, dribbling right onto my nipples as Heath lets out an *mmm*. Then the stream moves back down, more on my stomach... so hot and thick.

I know what's coming before it happens. I try to stay still at the next pan clank, but it's practically impossible as the ferocious heat of the liquid dribbles down onto my pussy. It really fucking burns.

I'm panting like crazy, muscles tense as I fight the pain. I can't stop a whimper as fingers seek out my clit and begin to tease me.

"Beautiful," Heath says. "Spread her wider, Josh, get ready for your starter."

Wider?! Jesus, it's going to burn so bad.

Josh splays my pussy lips and the pan clanks again. I grit my teeth hard, ready to be set on fire, but the pain gives way to pleasure in moments when it lands. Josh is there with a sweep of his pierced tongue in a millisecond, licking me clean.

"More, please," he says, and another dribble of heat lands, my pussy lips still splayed wide and vulnerable – but Josh's tongue is right there to save me from torture as he cleans me. His tongue keeps working, following the dribble of soup over my body wherever it goes. It's a clash of sensations that work beautifully together – the scorch of pain followed by Josh's horny, wet mouth.

Heath laughs when Josh starts sucking and lapping at my tits in a frenzy.

"Steady with the gobbling, Joshua. All three of us need to eat, remember?" I hear him step up to my head, with another clank of the pan. "Open your mouth, curva. Take your portion of soup. Your boyfriend is a great chef."

I know Josh is a great chef. He works wonders in the apartment while we cook together, serving up the most delicious meals, packed full of herbs and spices.

I open my mouth wide, and Heath is careful as he feeds me from the ladle. I recognise the taste. French onion – how fitting.

I'd love to give him a *yum* in appreciation, but I daren't. I hope that the way I open my mouth and stick my tongue out conveys my thanks. I'm like a fledgling chick, hungry as Heath dribbles more soup onto my tongue. He's so careful as he lets me savour and swallow.

"Good curva, only a touch of mess," Heath says, and his hair trails over me for a moment before his tongue sweeps around my lips and down my chin. "My turn now. I want my portion."

More heat. More ladles. More tongues. Two men licking soup from my naked body as I strain with the urge to arch and squirm for more. My skin lights up with desire, and I want the burn. I want the prickle of heat and the relief of hungry mouths in the aftermath. I want the agony of searing pain.

My thighs must be trembling when they return their attention to my pussy.

"Splay her wide," Heath says, "make sure that beautiful clit is standing proud."

I gasp when my pussy is splayed and Josh's mouth lands on my clit. It's so hard not to moan when he sucks and swirls his piercing.

"Let me see," Heath says.

One last hard flick with his piercing, and fuck, I'm sparking like I could burst into flames, desperate for more when my boyfriend's mouth leaves me.

"Such a gorgeous clit," Heath says, and fuck how I tense when he clanks the pan. "Do not clean her up until I say so, Joshua. Understand? I want our sweet curva to feel this one."

"Yes, sir," Josh says.

Heath clanks the pan again and I grit my teeth as the hot liquid hits with a searing heat that almost – *almost* – makes me fucking scream.

I'm panting, my tits heaving, my pussy on fucking fire.

Heath must have given Josh the nod because suddenly his face is buried, his tongue lapping at me, and fuck it's crazy how just like that I'm coming in his face, trying not to buck, trying to be still, trying to fucking breathe as my amazing boyfriend sucks the life out of me.

"Jesus," Heath says when Josh finally pulls away. "That was… hot."

Josh laughs. "Hotter for Ells than us. But yeah, so damn hot."

"Let's finish up," Heath says, "there's not much left."

I tense like a bitch when he clanks the pan again. But hell it's nice, as they take it in turns, slopping and lapping. So much soup over my body with hungry tongues licking me clean. I wonder if I'm a mess of gooey liquid, or nothing more than a slick, spit covered canvas. In a blindfold, I just can't tell.

"Almost done," Heath says, and the river of soup on my tits is a pure splosh as he empties the pan. They are tasting more than their yummy starter when they clean up the final portion. Teeth nip and tug my nipples, fingers kneading. Josh's fingers are back on my clit, circling, and my breaths are shallow, the taste of soup still in my mouth when Heath's lips land on mine. His tongue is after every last taste, digging around my cheeks as though I really am a soup bowl and he's licking me clean.

I could curse as the two guys disappear.

I want more soup, and I want more heat. More pain and pleasure. And more *them*.

Drawers are opened and closed in the kitchen area – more pots, pans and utensils. My mind reels, trying to guess what's coming next. Is it going to be another gloopy one? A stir fry? Noodles? Creamy pasta?

Seems it's not Josh who is the head chef tonight.

"Go wipe the table down," I hear Heath say, and footsteps sound in my direction.

I flinch when a spray of ice-cold water lands on my stomach with no warning whatsoever. I tense up, but Josh lays a hand on my leg.

"Tables don't move, *curva*," he reiterates, mimicking Heath's rich tone. "Make sure you stay still, no matter what."

I don't nod, just accept the spray as he soaks me all over. I grimace as he sprays a jet of water straight at my face, but I stay poised. *Professional.* My nipples must be bullet hard, my skin goosebumped when he splays my pussy lips and sprays three jets one after the other. Bastard.

A flannel lands and feels so good when he wipes me clean, paying special attention to my pussy as he dries me. I adore the fabric against my clit, and Josh knows it. He heightens the sensation on purpose, and trails the cloth up and over my nipples one after the other, enough to drive me wild.

Finally, he wipes my face clean.

I'm hoping he'll kiss me before heading back to the kitchen, but he doesn't, just walks away without a word.

There's an unmistakable sizzling sound as something hits a pan. Meat. Hot, fresh, sizzling meat. I hear the flip, before another sizzle, and I smell a searing steak in the pan. My stomach rumbles afresh, because I love steak – rare and tender. It's one of my favourites.

I'm nervous when footsteps approach again, because I can still hear the sizzle of the steak in the pan. I lay my palms flat to the tabletop and push down, clenching my stomach muscles.

"Here it comes, curva," Heath says, and I try to steady my breathing. It's going to be baking hot. Scorching. And no fucking shit, I get white behind my eyes when it lands on my ribs. It burns so bad I can barely breathe, taking every scrap of my resolve to stay still. I HAVE to stay still.

The steak must be rare, because I feel drizzles of liquid pooling in my bellybutton, and dribbling down my sides. The smell is enough to make my mouth water, despite my screaming skin.

Something pointed jabs my stomach, just a touch, and I flinch – instincts out of control. It's a knife. A fucking knife.

"Be very still now, Ella," Heath says. "I'll be very careful, but any wriggles from you are going to be a hazard."

He pokes me again, with the very tip of the blade, and I can't stop myself whimpering. The fear is primal. Impossible to battle.

"I'll forgive you that one," Heath says. "And I'll forgive you a nod or a shake of the head for this one, too. Do you trust me?"

I hesitate just a moment.

"Do you trust me, Ella, or do you wish to call off the proposal? The choice is yours. Yes, or no?"

My blood is pulsing through my ears, my instincts crying out NO, NO, NO, because I'll be a carving tray. My body will be a carving tray for a knife sharp enough to slice through steak, and slice through *me*, if he's not careful.

But do I trust him? Do I trust Heath?

I manage a nod.

Yes. I trust Heath.

I breathe in through my nose, and out through my mouth – slow breaths to take me away from the edge of panic. I'm going to be a carving tray for the *Count*. He's going to be cutting a blood-red steak on my body, with a blade sharp enough to slice through my skin.

But once my breathing calms and the panic eases just a touch, something else takes its place. Surrender. That beautiful subspace where I put myself in someone else's hands.

"Be still now, curva," Heath says, and I feel the steak moving on top of me. I feel the motion of the blade as Heath slices, so close to my skin. Sweeps of a knife that could make me bleed.

The serrated edge touches me, grazing gently before it's pulled away again to carve another slice. All my attention is on the way it feels, the sharpness of a metal blade as it lands and sweeps. The subspace consumes me, and in some deep-rooted part of my infatuation for extremity comes the crazy desire that Heath slips, and cuts.

"How about we give our platter some eyes?" Heath says, and his hands slip behind my head to take off my blindfold. I blink as I adjust to the light, then smile at the beautiful man up above me.

"Here, curva," he says, and the scent of steak wafts close to my face. "Open wide for your dinner."

My senses are skyrocketed to a whole new level now that I can see. I open my mouth for my reward, and Heath presents a chunk of meat for me. I chew on the piece of rare steak as he resumes slicing, and dare to look down, fascinated by the way Heath cuts. The knife looks so sharp. So dangerous.

I'm craving more of the blade than more of my dinner.

Josh laughs. "You look worse than a Nighttime Whispers victim." He trails his tongue up my belly, then takes a piece of steak in his mouth straight from my skin, chewing before he licks some more.

Heath feeds me as they eat, and his slicing gets more ferocious when he reaches my tits, where the final bulk of the steak is lying. I smile, wondering if maybe this is the point I get nicked or cut. The blade is crazy close to my nipples, and Heath teases me, flicking them with the side of the knife.

"Does that feel nice, curva?"

I don't speak. Don't nod. Just stay still and watch as the blade hovers so close to my stiff nipple.

"How about this?" He places the serrated blade on the very top of my nipple. I know he's controlling the weight of it when he slides the blade, touching just enough to make it prickle.

I thought my nipple couldn't get any harder, but the sensations are crazy good as my nipple pebbles and strains for more.

"Beautiful," Heath says before removing the knife and lowering his blood-stained lips to my tit, sucking my nipple in in one hard suck. Jesus fucking Christ!

He comes up for air, grabs a chunk of steak in his teeth and feeds me, kissing and biting at my mouth as we share the succulent treat.

"Simply divine," he says, licking his lips. "You may have the pleasure of the last piece," he says to Josh.

And it is a real pleasure as my man licks and sucks at my blood-stained tits before picking up the last piece of meat in his teeth, grinning at me as he brings it to my lips.

An amazing pleasure, chewing and kissing and licking at the juices.

With a final sweep of his tongue over my chin, Josh stands back.

"Wonderful," Heath says. "Our sweet curva looks like she's ready for dessert."

The guys retreat, and I wonder what's coming next. Josh is what comes next, armed with the spray bottle, filled with water. I get jetted again as he cleans up the *table* for round three, grinning at me as he does it.

I wish he would break the rules and make me come with the flannel. My clit is sparking with need, my adrenaline still pumping from the threat of the blade, and I want the release and I want more.

I want to feel a thin slice of a blade gone wrong. I want to feel the burn of it. I want to be the dirtiest most hardcore table girl there could be. My mind runs riot, spinning through the options, and I have to bite my lip so I don't moan when Heath arrives with bowls in his hands.

The cold jet of water Josh was using is nothing compared to the chill of the dessert Heath lays on my tits. Ice cream, thick and vanilla. He spoons it over my nipples, and down… down…

Josh's fingers splay my pussy without instruction and the freeze hits my clit, dribbling ice cream down my slit as it melts. I'm focused on trying not to shiver when Heath's fingers tilt my chin up.

"Open, curva, but don't swallow."

I adore the way our eyes meet as he pours thick double cream into my mouth, right to the brim. I breathe through my nose, keeping myself as still as I can.

I'm an ice cream covered whore with a mouth full of thick white topping, but it keeps on coming. Squirts of chocolate sauce, coating me in criss-crosses. Another stream down between my pussy lips. The chocolate smells so good. Oh, how I'd fucking love some.

"Don't swallow, curva," Heath says again, and eases my thighs apart. Josh splays my pussy wider and Heath holds up a spoon so I can see. "I know you like metal in your cunt, Ella. I'm sure you'll enjoy this."

A spoon.

A spoon in my cunt – big and round.

Oh my fucking God, Heath Mason is fucking my pussy with a metal spoon. I have to battle not to choke on my mouthful of cream.

"This is going to make the ice cream taste so much better," Heath says, pulling the spoon free from my pussy to scoop some up from my tits. Josh goes next, fucking me deep with his spoon before he takes a mouthful of vanilla. Then back to Heath. Both of them using my cunt as a dipping bowl before using my body as a plate. The ice cream is melting now, my bullet nipples feeling the creamy cold rivers as they run.

The guys' hot mouths land next, interspersed with spoons, and I'm lost to it. I can't move, can't make a sound, can't do anything but hold the sacred cream in my mouth like a good whore.

The chill of the air in the aftermath is almost worse than the shock of the chill I had when the ice cream landed. I'm cold now. Needy and tender, with my pussy crying out for more than just spoons. I want more metal inside me than that.

"Strawberry time," Josh says, and I have no chance of keeping the cream in my mouth without dribbling when he pushes a piece of ripe fruit inside.

My mouth is a dipping pot. Strawberry after strawberry as the men dip and eat from me.

But where is *my* dessert?

My pussy is hungrier than my stomach. *That's* where I want my dessert tonight.

Josh must read my mind.

"Keep that cream in your mouth," he tells me. "We're going to refill you, and you're a lucky girl. Two types of cream at once."

I can't stop myself gurgling when he takes my thighs and hauls me towards him. The cream in my mouth sloshes, and I fight the urge to retch when it hits the back of my throat. But the discipline is worth it. The moment Josh's swollen cock head glides its way along my gooey slit, I'm set for heaven.

The spoons had nothing on the barbells that pop their way in, one by one. He pumps me deep and fast, and for all my table pondering, I imagine how dirty they've been while I was a blindfolded player. Have they had their thick cocks set to burst all the while they've been eating? Have they been groping each other in the kitchen while they've been prepping the food?

It feels like it.

Josh doesn't go easy. He fucks me with all his might, with a pump, pump, pump, fucking pump until he pulls out. He's at my face in seconds, his knee on the tabletop beside me as he works his cock in his hand.

"Don't you dare fucking swallow," he says, and I groan as Heath takes position between my legs, slamming his thick barbelled shaft inside me as Josh blows his load right in my creamy mouth.

More cream.

Fuck yeah, I want it.

"Dirty girl," Josh says and drops his face to mine. He licks my open lips, then dips his tongue inside, playing with the gooey mix of cum and cream. I don't kiss him, just leave my mouth open wide, shunted back and forth as Heath pistons between my legs.

Oh, yeah. I want Heath's cream in my mouth, too. I'm such a greedy slut.

Heath takes longer than Josh, gripping and groping my messy tits as he works himself up to shoot his load. He's hitting the spot so well, and Josh's mouth is so horny that I can't hold back from coming myself, only I have to be still and silent through mine. I have to obey the instructions.

It's so fucking hard.

The ripples that rock through me are intensified beyond belief by the way I have to clench my muscles to stay still. I close my eyes, wishing I could swallow and cry out, but it's forbidden. This is a proposal. No matter what the situation, this is a proposal, and I'm an entertainer.

Heath doesn't come inside me. Instead, Josh pulls away enough to let Heath angle his swollen cock at my mouth, working himself until his jets of cum add to the messy churn in my mouth.

Three loads of cream in one. Salty and sweet.

Heath dips his tongue in for a swirl, and it's still dripping white when he rises. He kisses my boyfriend as I stare up at them, mute as they eat each other's mouths out like partners in crime.

Or just partners.

They look like partners as they kiss. Heath takes Josh's face in his hands, groaning with passion, and I may as well be nothing more than a table when Josh tangles his fingers in Heath's hair right back.

It's absolutely fucking beautiful.

They both have puffy lips when they finally turn their attention back to me.

Heath strokes a thumb across my cheek.

"You can swallow now, curva. Enjoy your dessert."

It's such a glorious relief when I do. What a fucking treat for me. I'd give them a *thank you*, if I was allowed to.

The guys scoop up the remnants of melted ice cream and globs of chocolate, and let me suck their fingers clean. Josh makes me retch on his, diving right to the back of my throat with chocolate sauce – and that starts a game that makes them grin like a filthy pair of jokers. Who can get their fingers the deepest, trying to make me retch on more and more thick gloopy goodness.

I'm such a good girl that I take both of them. They can have my throat. They can jab as deep as they want, but they won't make me break my role.

Or so I think until Josh starts up, teasing my clit with his chocolate coated fingers.

"How much chocolate do you want, baby? How about some of Heath's? Would you like that?"

My breaths quicken.

Josh looks at Heath.

"I think she wants some extra chocolate dip, don't you?"

"Hmm… she's welcome to some."

"Go on, give it to her. Give it to your dirty curva."

Heath hitches himself onto the table, so close I can see him spread his ass. His fingers are already messy with chocolate when he slides three into his asshole.

Josh works my clit, slow and steady.

"Give her that yummy chocolate," Josh says, and his voice is laced with filth.

Josh wants it as much as I do. He wants to see me suck on Heath's filthy fingers, straight from his asshole.

Heath gets down from the table before he presents his filthy fingers to my open mouth. He runs them around my lips, smiling at me.

"Let's go real deep," he says, and drives his fingers deep, curving into my throat, and pinches my nose with his free hand as he does it.

He fucks my throat with his dirty fingers, and I can't stop choking. I can't breathe if I don't.

"Suck," he says. "Suck like a good girl."

I suck him like a good girl, with my nose still pinched.

I clean Heath Mason's filthy fingers like they are the most delicious delicacy in the world.

And I come against my boyfriend's fingers as I do it.

"That was everything I hoped it would be and more," Heath says as he helps me down from the table. "And once again, look at the mess we've made. Always so filthy with our playtime."

He's not wrong. The table is a mess and so am I.

"It was amazing," I say.

"Ditto that," Josh says and I'm pulled into a group hug that feels so damn good.

I feel so damn good.

And I feel even better than good when my guys lead me to the shower and the pair of them lather me up, and it feels like I've died and gone to heaven, my two gorgeous gods, pampering me.

I don't want this holiday to end.

eight

"Let's at least have breakfast first, Ella," Heath says, as I follow him and Josh through to the kitchen, but I'm not interested in pancakes and blueberries right now.

All I want is Nighttime Whispers.

Heath's bed may well be the most comfortable in the world – me cosy, alongside the two men dreams are made of – but I could hardly sleep a wink last night. I'm so excited for my reward.

"How many episodes can I watch?" I ask, picturing myself in Heath's cinema room with a load of popcorn and the lead performer beside me. It's going to be so amazing, it's insane.

"As many as you want to watch. I have the full collection, and some outtakes."

I groan as he takes out the pancake pan.

"Now you're just tormenting me! I'll want to watch them all. Every single one."

"I'm not tormenting you. You can binge watch, that's fine with me. Just so long as you're ready for the next proposal this evening."

I tip my head. "You're going to binge watch them with me? All of them?"

He laughs. "That would be tormenting me. I've lived through that season for months. I know every line by heart." There's a twinkle in his eye when he looks at me. "But I'll tolerate another rerun for you, sweet curva. You deserve it after last night."

I'm so glad I was such a good table. Thank fuck I passed the test.

"You're watching too, aren't you?" I ask Josh, and my boyfriend shrugs, trying to be nonchalant as he grabs the blueberries and cream from the fridge.

"Maybe." He looks at Heath. "See how many *I* can tolerate."

He's fooling around. He can play casual all he wants, but I know the truth. He's almost as desperate to see Heath vamped up on screen as I am.

I get the plates as the guys prep breakfast – virtually hopping from foot to foot with impatience. I gobble my pancake stack on the terrace as quickly as I can while they savour theirs. I'm such an idiot, but I can't help it. Blueberries or Nighttime Whispers? The answer is obvious. The sun is glorious, and the pool looks inviting as hell in this heat, but I want the darkness of the cinema room. I *need* to know what happens!

I practically sprint back through to the kitchen once Josh and Heath put their knives and forks down, loading up the dishwasher on a mission.

It's still pretty early... all twelve episodes will take a nine-hour binge watch, but that's alright. It'll leave us time for a proposal, if we get going now.

"Pleaseeeeeeee," I say, my hands in a prayer position as I race back out to the loungers. "Come on, Heath! Let's get started!"

His eyes are so gorgeous as they fix on mine, and he gives me his *Count* smile on purpose. "Go on then, grab a drink and some snacks, then get to the cinema room. Choose your view."

I ballerina twirl on my way back through the villa, my heart racing on overdrive as I stop at the snack cupboard. Heath actually has popcorn. For real. Salted and sweet, or coated caramel. I take both, and load up my arms with Coke cans.

If any of the millions of fans around the world could see me now, they would be so jealous, it's insane. They'd lynch me for a shot at this.

It's obvious which one of the seats I'm going to pick in the cinema room. Right at the centre in the second row. Prime viewing position. I tap my foot, wondering what is taking so long as I wait for the two of them to join me. I really need to know what the hell is going to happen this series. I've been thinking about it for months now. I know every single character by heart – every plot twist, every chase and bite. Everything. But so does Josh... he's often on the sofa beside me, pretending to be more interested in pizza and scrolling than he is at staring at *Count* Heath. But that's bullshit. He's invested too.

He can put on as much of a front as he likes, but it won't fool me.

I'm already sipping on a can of Coke when the two loverboys finally make their appearance, and oh fuck. FUCK. They've checked out of their shorts and t-shirt look. They're dressed up to the max – thank you, aircon. Both of them are dressed up for the viewing, and I mean seriously dressed up.

Heath is in a suit! One of the Count's fucking suits, with the burgundy neck tie!

I'm open mouthed as he approaches.

He's brushed his hair dead straight and walks towards me with his hands behind his back – casual Count style.

I squeak, I'm so excited. I clap my hands with an *oh my God!*

"Rewards are rewards," he says, and takes a seat beside me. "You don't earn them easily, and you deserve the full experience when you do."

I shrug with a laugh. "How am I supposed to focus on the screen with you looking like that?!"

Josh clears his throat as he takes a seat on my opposite side.

"Excuse me, *curva*." He's smirking. "Turn your attention away from the vamp icon for a second please, will you?"

Fuck, I've been so caught up in the Count that I didn't notice just how styled Josh is for the occasion, too. I've seen him in suits plenty of times, since he practically lives in them for work, but this one is different up close. He's wearing a Nighttime Whispers style suit like Heath is. Not the same necktie, but a brocaded waistcoat under a jacket.

"Well, well, well. I'm one hell of a lucky girl," I say, and give my boyfriend a kiss. "Two vamps for the price of one. I know you've got a bite on you too, Josh."

Heath squeezes my knee. "Are you sure you want a premier today? Or shall we get into some real-life action?"

"That's not fair!" I giggle. "I want BOTH!"

He licks his lips. "Maybe you'll be an even luckier girl than you think you are. But in the meantime." He takes a remote control from his jacket pocket and switches the massive screen on. "Time for episode one."

I get shivers as the screen lights up. The familiar haunting theme tune of Whispers sounds out, roaring through the incredible speakers, and there he is. The Count, turning to face the camera with his beautifully evil smile on his face. Bats flock around his head, then zoom away, and the camera pans to the village of Kington Springs, surrounded by woodland.

My heart speeds up, wondering what will happen to Polly Anna, and there she is, too. Right from the off.

She's running, just like she was in the cliffhanger, her breaths choking as she runs, exhausted. She stumbles over a fallen branch and takes a frantic look around her. Jeez, he must be close by. He's always so fast in the woods.

I stiffen, listening as she pants. My eyes must be as wide as hers as I watch, already consumed by the tension. A crack of a branch behind her, and she's off again with a whimper, trying to sprint. But she's tired. Too tired to run. So she hides, pressing her back to a nearby tree trunk in the shadows as the crackle of branches grows closer.

"Oh, Polly… where are you, Polly?" The Count's laugh is so cold. "You can run, darling, but you'll never escape. You belong to me now."

Polly Anna has been in love with the Count since she first arrived at Kington Springs, but she didn't know his true nature then. No one in the village ever speaks about it.

Polly closes her eyes, and I feel her internal struggle. Fighting the urge of passion. Her heart belongs to the Count, but her head is screaming no.

I get that.

And I also get her curse of frustration.

I understand how hard it would be to run from someone you want so bad, even if it leads to your own demise.

Someone like Heath as well as the character he plays.

"Accept your fate, Polly," the Count says. "We both know where your road leads."

His shadow shows on the screen, approaching her so slowly. Stalking her like a wolf after a lamb.

She grabs a branch from the ground and leaps out to confront him in the moonlight.

"Stay away from me! This isn't fate calling me, it's *you*."

"I *am* your fate. I'm the one who controls your destiny."

"Yeah?" She steps backwards. "And what is that? You're going to drink the life out of me and leave me here to rot, are you? Like so many others." Her eyes brim with tears. "Don't think I don't know. The village can keep secrets, but the woodland can't. I can virtually hear the ghosts all around me. People you killed, you evil bastard."

The Count tips his head, smirking like Heath does. The moonlight through the trees catches his gorgeous face perfectly.

"Oh, I can hear all of the ghosts around here. Every single one of them. I've been slaying people and setting their souls free for centuries. So many poor victims." He looks so evil, toying with her. "Some struggle and fight. Some wilt like flowers. Some welcome me with open arms."

I know that. I've seen his massacres and chases through every series.

Polly jabs the branch in his direction, like that will ever deter him. "And which do you prefer, you sick fuck?"

He shrugs. "That depends on the victim."

"What about me? How do you think I'm going to go? I'll fight to the death, I swear it!"

The Count is such a bastard, he laughs at her.

"That branch is hardly going to be a stake through my heart, Polly. Come! Wilt like a flower in my open arms."

He opens his arms, and I want to be Polly Anna. I'd love to be that terrified, staring at the monster while he coaxes me in.

Her lip trembles as the tears start up. Her blonde hair is so pretty, her stunning pink dress from the gala torn to shreds.

"At least let me say my goodbyes before you leave me here as an empty corpse. I've only been in the village a few months, but that doesn't mean I don't care. It doesn't mean people don't care about *me*."

"You don't need to say any goodbyes. The moment you ran from the hall, everyone knew you were doomed to my will."

I see the pain in her eyes. Her friendships shattered at the realisation that nobody tried to save her.

"You were doomed from the moment we locked eyes across Church Street, and everybody knew it." The Count pauses. "Everyone except you."

"This place is sick."

"This is the place you chose to call your home."

"But I didn't know then…"

He steps closer. "Be honest, Polly. If you had have known, would you have turned away?"

Fuck, he's got her. Her face tells the truth, because even now, she can't resist him. I know that feeling in the flesh these days, not just on the screen. Heath may not be a vampire, but he's got the same thrall. The same mesmeric beauty.

"Come," the Count says. "Come to me and be the wilting flower. Enjoy being the petals in my arms."

"For you to scatter me in the dirt when you're done?"

His fangs are long now – stunning and pointed. I get a bout of goosebumps, imagining them biting down on my tit.

Polly sobs, and fucking hell, I can't believe it. She's been in the past two series. I like her. Surely she's not going to die in episode one? I almost turn to Heath, but I don't want spoilers. I CAN'T have spoilers.

She drops the branch when he closes the distance, wilting against his suited body as he takes hold of her arms. His teeth graze her neck as he smells her fear.

"I'm not going to scatter you in the dirt. Not tonight. You're going to go home."

She stiffens. "What?"

He laughs as he nips his teeth, just a touch.

"You're free to go, Polly. You're not going to be a ghost in the woods. Not this time."

Her expression is incredible. She's so confused, it's palpable. Katie Ryan really is an amazing actress.

"But I thought..."

"Thought, thought, thought. So many assumptions. Always so many assumptions in this *godforsaken* place."

"But when you chased me..."

I adore the Count's laugh.

"Even vampires like to have a little fun sometimes."

This is new. The Count is normally so brutal. I mean, I knew Polly was going to be different, because his stone cold heart had warmed to her, but this is new turf. I glance at Heath, and he's smirking at the screen, not at me.

"No spoilers," he says.

I watch the Count walk away from Polly, leaving her like a terrified doll in the darkness. He strolls and she watches, transfixed.

"Are you coming, or not?" he asks, casting a glance over his shoulder. "If you want to trek back to the village alone, that's fine by me."

"I, uh..."

He holds out a hand, his fangs still long and glinting under the moonlight.

"Come with me, or muddle your way along the path with the ghosts. Your call."

She picks up the courage to walk towards him, and her character returns as she calms, walking along at his side.

"I thought *you* were in charge of my destiny, not me."

"I still am."

"Really? What if I choose to pack up and leave Kington? I could pack a suitcase and be out of here."

The way he looks at her is intoxicating.

"You won't leave. You won't so much as pack a thing."

And from the way he looks at her, it's obvious. She won't pack up and leave. Not even now she knows the truth – that the Count is a vampire who controls the whole village.

"Time for popcorn," Josh says as the scene changes, and hands over the caramel coated pack. He grins when I take it from him. "Jeez, Ells, honestly. You're sucked in so bad it's hilarious."

"Interesting choice of words," Heath says from my other side, and I jump as he lunges at me with his mouth open wide. But he's only fucking joking. He nips at my shoulder, then pulls away, taking a handful of popcorn on his way.

I can't help but be kinda disappointed.

Josh is right, I am sucked in by the new series. The episodes zoom by, and I fire questions at Heath like there's no tomorrow every time the credits roll. I am right back in Kington Springs, watching the tension between Polly and the Count grow and unfold now she knows the truth.

In this new round of episodes he ghosts a whole load more visitors in the woodland, and reveals the sacred past of Mackay, and by the time the finale approaches and the outside hunters arrive to interrogate Polly, she chooses crazy loyalty for the man who makes her bleed for fun. Because he does make her bleed for fun. A lot.

I groan when the end scene appears, knowing how the next cliffhanger is going to unfold.

The hunters have Polly as a ransom. Of course they do.

And will the Count surrender, really?

How the fuck is he going to rescue her from the swarms of bounty hunters in the village if he doesn't?

"No spoilers," Heath says before I get the chance to ask him. "The next part of the plot is strictly confidential."

"Just a clue! Please!"

He shakes his head, and damn him, he's insanely smoking hot in his Count getup. I'm as devoted to him as the woman on the screen.

"Come on, Heath, just a teaser!"

He zips his mouth. "My lips are sealed."

I groan, because there's no way he's going to reveal anything. His adherence to confidentiality is as solid as Josh's.

"Bloopers, then. You said there were outtakes. Come on, I'm desperate!"

"You really want to watch the bloopers after the grand finale of the series?"

"Um, YES."

Josh leans in. "Heath, that's the most ridiculous question I've ever heard. She'd watch every scene from every possible angle if she could."

Heath laughs. "Yes, I can see that, *genius*. Maybe I'm just keen to hear her enthusiasm."

"Hear her beg, you mean?"

"I'll beg," I butt in. "Happily. No problem."

"Let's save any begging for later." Heath flicks the remote. "Outtakes it is."

It's so bizarre to see scenes with the word *cut* sounding out amidst the action. I've watched plenty of online videos of people on the set, with candid snippets, but nothing as professional as this. These are outtakes from the actual filming.

I almost piss myself laughing when Heath trips up on a woodland branch, going sprawling into the undergrowth, fully suited. He scrambles to his feet, and his pristine shirt is covered in mud. The way he swipes it down as the cast laugh around him is spectacular. *Fuck sake, everyone, it's not you who has to go back to wardrobe!*

There are plenty of blooper scenes where people goof up their lines, or get the giggles, but there are a set of them that have me transfixed. One of the woodland scenes where Polly Anna *falls* into the Count's arms.

Hmm. She seems to *fall* too hard on quite a few occasions, although she passes it off as slipping on her heels. I see the way she looks at him – still in the character of Polly while Heath straightens her up. She giggles a tad too much. Giving him the eye like he's still the Count, drawn to her for all eternity.

"She fancies you," I say. "You do know that, right?"

"Katie? Yes. I know that."

I raise my eyebrows. "Are you not tempted? She's absolutely gorgeous."

"No, I'm not tempted."

"Really?"

Josh squeezes my knee. "There are plenty of stunners on set,

Ells. I'm sure they're all out to tempt the *Count*, not just Katie Ryan. He could be a very busy boy if he wanted to."

I examine the *Count* at my side. There's no doubt that he must be a megastar of magnetism on set, not just off it. Yeah, he could be a very busy boy indeed, but here he is, isolated in France, with two hookers.

"You don't fancy anyone on set at all?" I ask him. "What about Victoria Pewter? She looks quite like me. Or Peter Harold? He'd look like Josh if you squinted."

"It's not that I don't fancy them, I don't want them," Heath says, and there's an edge to his voice. Almost defensive. "I spend my life living out drama through filming every day, I don't want any drama outside of it."

Ouch. Something has spiked him. Josh nudges my foot and I let go of the conversation, taking another handful of popcorn and turning my attention back to the screen.

"Sorry," Heath says, out of nowhere.

I smile at him. "You've got nothing to be sorry for. I shouldn't be asking. It's none of my business, I just get excited by Whispers. Everyone onscreen is amazing. Especially Polly. And you, of course."

"Oh shit," Heath says as the scene changes. "My life flashed before my eyes with this one."

Polly Anna wakes in her bed, shocked to see a shadowy figure standing over her. She makes a run for it and the chase is on yet again, the evil Count Valenti desperate for his fill.

"The director insisted on one fluid take," Heath says. "I really thought we'd nailed it, until I screwed up at the end."

I'm entranced, my heart racing as the Count races after Polly, the cameraman close behind.

Polly is screeching and flailing and throwing whatever she can grab at as she makes her escape into the street outside. But the Count is too quick. He grabs her and slams her up against the church door. Polly is panting hard and so am I, her tits heaving in her lowcut nightdress, the lucky bitch. What I would give for Count Valenti to chase me like that.

The camera zooms in on Polly's pale neck and the Count shows his fangs before biting down.

Polly struggles at first, then goes limp in his arms as he sucks her blood.

"Wait for it," Heath says.

All of a sudden, the Count is coughing – no – he's choking, doubling over, can't breathe.

Polly – or rather Katie, springs to life, grabs him from behind and performs the Heimlich manoeuvre. I'm gasping and nearly choking on my popcorn as Heath's pale face turns purple.

"Dear fucking God," I say, just as Katie gives a final thrust and something flies from Heath's mouth.

People swarm the set. Someone – I think it's the director – picks up whatever it was that flew from Heath's mouth.

"Fucking hell, Heath," he says, "you could have fucking died if it wasn't for Katie's quick thinking. Are you alright?"

Count Valenti is getting his breath back, leaning on Katie against the church door.

"Let's take five and then we'll go again," the director says and the scene ends.

"It took another three takes before he was satisfied," Heath says.

"What the hell happened?" I ask.

"Fake blood capsule. I'm supposed to hide it under my tongue once I've broken it with my teeth. But somehow it went down my throat, probably because I was breathing too hard after the chase."

"That was scary," I say.

"Indeed," Heath says. "Quite ironic that Polly saved me."

It's mad that I feel jealous of Polly – or Katie.

"Yeah, well done, Polly," I say.

We watch the rest of the outtakes, and I'm laughing afresh by

THE NAUGHTY WEEK

the end, clapping my hands as Katie really fluffs up a village store scene as Polly. She doubles up, pissing herself laughing with a *sorry, ARGH!*

It's a shame to see the reel ending. I could watch this stuff for days.

Heath's smirk is back on his face when the lights come on in the room.

"So, would you still enjoy being Polly, owned by the Count now that you have seen the bloopers?" he asks me.

Fuck, Heath's eyes bore into mine, and I *am* Polly, staring into his vampire beauty.

"That's another ridiculous question from you, *Count*."

"Yes, and another one where I want to hear your enthusiasm."

I twist towards him. "I'd love to be Polly, even for just one millisecond. It would be absolutely fucking amazing. AMAZING."

"Good to hear, since you may just get the chance," he says, and drops an envelope in my lap.

The proposal envelope...

"Josh may have had a spoiler or two about this one," Heath says, and winks at my boyfriend.

I look between the two of them – two conspiratorial fuck buddies, beyond irresistible in their suits. Heath's sizing must fit Josh perfectly, because Josh definitely didn't have that garb in his suitcase when we left London.

"Go on," Josh says, smirking as dirtily as Heath. "Open the envelope, *curva*. The Count controls your destiny too, after all."

Yes, he does.

Heath Mason controls every scrap of my destiny with this envelope in my hands.

He's welcome to it.

nine

TUESDAY

Nighttime Whispers doesn't need to be limited to the TV screen this evening, sweet curva. The Count is in my blood now, as I've played the character for so long.
And the Count knows how to chase and terrify his victims.
Tonight, I will be lucky enough to have an extremely skilled assistant. Someone who can also run, chase and capture. I'm sure we'll both be trying our very best to win the game of hide and seek.
Once we catch you, you will be at the mercy of the Count.
Finally, Ella, you will have the chance to be Polly Anna, and your 'fate' will belong to me.

Proposal duration – three hours.
Reward – some more competition time for Joshua tomorrow. I know you love a good squash game, darling. You'll have earnt it.

Heath Mason playing a squash match with Josh? I have no idea how that will pan out, but if I had to hedge my bets...

Josh is one of the most competitive people I've ever met when it comes to any kind of sport, especially one on one. No, scrap that. He's *the* most competitive person I've ever met.

I didn't have a clue Heath liked sport. I gathered he must like something, to keep a physique like his, but I'd never figured what.

"Squash?" I ask our client. "I didn't realise you liked that kind of thing."

"*That kind of thing?* Sport, you mean?" He smiles. "I'm very fond of a good game. I used to be at the top of our local squash league when I was growing up. Unfortunately, playing is a lot less enjoyable when you have a thousand cameras in your face whenever you leave the house." He points at the floor. "That's why I have a court downstairs. But I only usually practice solo."

"A court downstairs? A squash court? Here?"

"And a pool table, dartboard, and gym setup, yes."

Well that wasn't on the villa tour. I wonder how much about this place is behind closed doors...

"You look surprised," Heath says, and I shrug.

"No, it makes sense, it's just..."

"Just what? You can't imagine vampires with a squash racquet in their hand? It definitely wouldn't look so fitting on the screen." He squeezes my shoulder. "Yes, Ella, I enjoy plenty of sport, just like Joshua. We just don't get the opportunity to be gym buddies all that often."

The way Josh smirks and nods at him only reinforces just how little I truly know about Heath.

"That's quite a reward," Josh says. "Can't wait. Finally."

"Yes, finally."

There's a look that lingers between them, and gives me a rollercoaster lurch. It's clear all over again. I'm in the dark about almost everything Heath related compared to the way Josh knows him.

And I'll be literally in the dark tonight, it seems.

Even the thought of the upcoming proposal gives me shivers after our Nighttime Whispers binge.

"Where are you going to chase me?" I ask Heath, switching the topic. "Nowhere public, obviously."

"There is plenty of space here," he says. "The grounds are probably bigger than you're aware of, having spent so much of your holiday so far basking on the terrace."

"And in the pool," I add, then raise an eyebrow. "And naked, remember?"

He nods, flashing me his Count smile. "Oh yes, you've spent plenty of time naked, and that won't change tonight. Once we've captured you."

"Hmm." I sit back in my seat. "What about if *I* win? Is there a clause for that? Do you get a time limit on how long you have to capture me? You are playing competitive sports together as a reward after all."

"We never negotiate with proposals, remember?" Josh says, but I shrug.

"They aren't usually delivered in person. I can make an exception just once, right?"

"I like that idea, actually," Heath says. "What do you think, Josh? Twenty minutes?"

"Twenty minutes?" Josh looks right at me. "Easy peasy. We'll catch her way quicker than that."

"Oi," I give his arm a jokey slap. "You're underestimating me."

"We'll soon find out."

"And if I win?" I ask my boyfriend.

"It's up to the *Count*, it's his proposal after all."

We both look at Heath.

"If you win, we'll drink champagne and toast your success. Happy days."

I laugh. "You're making me want to lose now!"

"Let's see if you're still saying that once the chase is underway."

I don't break a sweat at this kind of event like I would have done when I first became an entertainer. I've been chased before during proposals, by complete strangers in extreme circumstances. I know the adrenaline and instinctive panic that comes when I'm trying my best to run and hide. I've been chased through wooded paths and bundled into the back of a van. I've been chased through a derelict house, trying to hide in dark corners. And all the while, I've loved it – even though my body has been screaming the opposite.

I've never been chased by Josh though. Not yet…

And I've definitely never been chased by the Count.

What an honour. I'm going to give it everything I've got. Show these guys how unwilling a victim I can be.

We eat dinner together first, with both gorgeous men still dressed in their finest attire. A delicious stir fry as the first bottle of tonight's champagne flows. I watch the sky darkening through the windows amidst the chatter, and my instincts are already spiking as we put our plates in the dishwasher.

"What do you want your *victim* to be wearing for the chase?" I ask Heath.

"I'll leave that up to you. We'll leave you alone for thirty minutes, during which time you can prepare yourself and begin your escape."

"Thirty minutes. Cool."

I'd set an alarm on my phone if I had access to it, but the clocks around the villa will have to do. The minutes counting down will be palpable as they rise in intensity.

"Your time starts now," Heath says, and I don't waste a second, darting through to the bedroom and looking through my collection of clothing. What will live up to the *Count's* attire? Uh, nothing. Not when he's dressed like that. But I'll try my best.

I packed some of my finest evening attire to bring along to France with me, so I pick one from the collection. A trailing black dress, low cut with a side split up to my thigh. I'll be able to run fine in that, and I'm going to go barefoot, so heels don't hinder me.

I don't spend long on my makeup – just outline my eyes in my trademark cat flicks, and put on my finest scarlet lipstick. Then I check the time on Heath's bedside clock. Only ten minutes left for the proposal to get underway.

And for me to get away.

When I leave the bedroom, the place is in total darkness. The guys have switched off all of the lights. Every single one of them. I wonder where they are. Are they close by, in the darkness? Will they be able to hear me make my move? It makes the situation so much more ominous that I freeze by the door, listening for movements, or breaths. But there is nothing. Only silence.

I don't know the villa well enough yet to dash freely, and I won't be giving away my location by hitting any light switches. I make my way carefully through to the kitchen, reaching out for the familiar anchor of the breakfast bar to orientate myself. The moonlight is strong outside, but it isn't reaching me here in the kitchen. I'm in the shadows. I use the opportunity to take some deep breaths as I contemplate my route. What will the guys expect me to do? Race into unknown territory on the outskirts of the villa grounds, or stay close by for an up-close game of hide and seek?

But the real question is… what do I *want* to do?

My feet answer the question for me, itching to run, run, run. So that is what I do. I dash straight for the door onto the terrace, easing the handle open as quietly as I can before I skirt alongside the loungers with my back against the wall. I follow the angle of the wall at the end, and in the moonlight I see the relaxation room where we had our pamper session. How ironic. This is anything but a pamper session. My heart is thumping, the adrenaline starting to flow, and I enjoy that. The terror. I let my mind race through the chase scenes in Nighttime Whispers – so many victims lost and succumbing to the Count's fangs in their neck once he reaches his prey.

I sink into the zone. I'm Polly Anna. And I'm on the run.

From the man she loves.

From the *men* she loves.

Oh fuck, I should never use that term in the plural.

I make a dash for the relaxation room, my breaths already hitching as I reach the other side. The grounds around Heath's huge villa are flat, with perfect grass and high walls around the outside. I can navigate this. I reach the boundary wall and race along the outskirts, unsure of quite what lies up ahead. My preparation time must be long gone by now – the chase underway – and I speed up, my feet silent as I run. I can hear the sea beyond the wall, and I ache to be in there, wading in and racing through the waves as my two assailants charge after me in floods of water. I'd love the sand beneath my toes, my feet pelting as I sprint, but I can't go out there. For now, it has to be the grounds.

I feel as though I'm in the middle of nowhere within minutes – the huge villa a block of magnificence, lit up in the moonlight before my eyes. And I realise this was a bullshit move. I have nowhere to hide here. Nothing but open ground.

Crap.

I'll be fallen prey in no time if I stay here.

I have no choice but to make a run for it. Three, two, one, and I go for it, sprinting with everything I've got. It's a relief when I reach a corner at the rear of the villa. I haven't been here before, but that's ok. I can make it around to the other side if I'm calm and steady. I breathe in through my nose and out through my mouth, dipping down as I pass each window, and leaping past the floor to ceiling panes. The villa really is massive. The circuit feels endless.

I scout around for a glimpse of anything that could hide me, and that's when I catch sight of one of the guys across the lawn, by the boundary wall. Jesus, how my stomach lurches. From this distance, I don't know which of the two it is. I stay statue still until they are out of sight, and keep going on my way. I brace myself, prepared to be leapt on at any second, but as I turn another corner, there is nobody there.

My feet hit tiles again, and ahead of me, I see the gates of the main entrance.

It gives me a lurch of recognition – the excitement as our cab pulled up and dropped us at our destination. It's only been a few days but it feels like a lifetime ago.

Fuck it. I take a chance at heading straight in through the front door, trying to ease it open. And YES! It moves. It lets me in.

I feel like a chase professional as I complete my circuit, right back to the breakfast bar. I toy with the idea of disappearing back into the bedroom and hiding out where I started. The clock must have been ticking fast while I've been outside. I wonder how far away I am from the win…

I think maybe, just maybe, I'll do it…

Until I hear footsteps behind me, charging fast from the dining table. Oh my fucking God, I shriek as the figure thumps into the opposite side of the breakfast bar and lunges over for me. And of course I have no fucking idea which of the pair this is, because he's masked! In a Venetian style devil mask that looks ominous as fuck in the shadows.

That's when the true instinct of terror hits me. It's inescapable. Beyond rational thought.

I escape with a screech, racing with everything I have towards the doors to the terrace, knowing the masked figure is right behind me. I'm past the loungers when I see my second masked assailant on the other side of the pool, waiting for me.

Two masked assailants, in period style attire. It gives an edge of swords, teeth and ravaged corpses.

Nighttime Whispers.

I'm scissored in this position, with nowhere to go. There is no chance in hell that I will make it past the pair of them, so my decision is made in a heartbeat.

I hold my skirt as I run and leap straight into the pool, spluttering as I resurface to find the two men watching me. One at each set of steps.

"I'm not getting out!" I screech. "I'm not giving in! Forget it!"

"Oh, curva," Heath's voice sounds out. "Do you really think that's going to stop us?"

I paddle in the centre of the pool, spinning as I tread water.

My blood is pumping, and my senses are reeling, my dress billowing out around me as I contemplate just what the fuck I'm going to do from here. A standoff, really?

But they answer the question for me.

Both men walk down the pool steps, not giving a toss for their suits as they enter the water. I'm a fucking fish being hunted as I flail for the edge to haul myself out, but I don't make it. Two pairs of hands land on me and yank me hard away from the side.

I kick and lash out, beyond control as I try to get away from them. Fight or flight. Both screaming in my veins.

"Give in, curva," Heath says, his grip firm on my arm, but I shake my head.

"No! Never!"

"Really?" I hear Josh's voice. "Let's see about that, shall we?"

I'm not prepared for the brutality of his hands when he shoves me under the water. I have no warning to take a breath, so the water chokes me, and I battle. Holy fuck, how I battle. But it doesn't make any difference.

Josh lets me up for some gulps of air, and I blink and stare at the both of them towering over me, with their tailored suits soaked to their skin.

"Do you submit?" Heath asks, but fuck them, no!

I shake my head, kicking out at their legs until Josh shoves me right back under the water.

Both pairs of hands hold me under this time. I'm trapped. Truly trapped. Being at their mercy doesn't even cut it.

I hold my breath, and the reality hits. I've been chased and captured, bound and beaten, but never fucking drowned before. I've never known the terror that comes from being held under water and unable to breathe. It's a different sensation, being deprived of air.

It makes me fight harder. Desperate.

I'm choking and spluttering, gasping for deep breaths when they let me to the surface for the second time.

"Do you submit now?" Heath asks, laughing in his deep, vampiric tone.

"Fuck you!" I yell, insanity taking over. "No!"

Their attire makes it so easy for me to *be* Polly Anna, flaming with the fight. But it's hard to be Polly Anna while I'm underwater for the third time, flailing with all my might but still powerless to get to the surface.

Again, they raise me. Again, I say no. I won't submit!

I try kicking, punching, fighting, but none of it works. The plunges get longer, deeper, until I'm heady with the need for air. My lungs are hurting, my muscles are aching… and subspace is truly calling.

They let me up onto my back this time, so I'm floating – my tits bobbing as I retch then gulp for air. Heath's hand clutches my throat, and Josh grabs my tits and squeezes hard.

"Still after some more?" Josh asks, and Heath responds before I can, using his grip on my neck to push just my head back under the water. My eyes are open, and I can see them both through the ripples, tall shadows above me. I blow out bubbles of air, shocked when a hand slides up my thigh to my pussy, and grinds against my slit while I'm powerless to breathe.

Even now, in this position, it feels so good.

It makes it so much easier to be at their mercy…

The fight is all pretend the next time they let me up for a few desperate breaths. I grit my teeth and open my legs wider as they force my face back under the water. My eyes are stinging and my ears are ringing, but my pussy is needier than ever.

I don't know how long I last while they toy with me – cutting off my air as they tease my clit. One of them yanks my dress down to free my floating tits, not giving a shit if they damage the fabric. My nipples are exposed, and they use them. They hurt them. They use my body as they drown and choke me, but even through the screaming panic I feel inside, I'm desperate for more.

"Do you submit?" Heath asks again, and this time I smile at him.

"I submitted a long time ago."

"You enjoy being a drowned little plaything?" he asks, and slaps my wet tits.

"I guess so."

"She likes any filthy thing," Josh says. "Even being starved of air."

This is a whole new kind of breath play. One that's not even on the naughty list it's so fucking weird. Being drowned over and over in a swimming pool, after being chased down by two suited men out for my blood.

Heath keeps me in position as Josh disappears to the side of the pool. My boyfriend reaches for my arms when he's out, and drags me out of the water like a drowned rat – a heaving, retching mess as I get dumped on my back on the tiles.

"You're going to pay for your fight now, curva," Heath says as he climbs out after us. "You made us get fucking wet for you."

"Yeah. And you made me wet for you, you sick fucks. Call us even."

"Still got some fight in you, haven't you?" Josh says, and puts his shoe on my tits. I really have made these guys soaking wet. His brogue is dripping. "Let's get that fight out and away."

They take an arm each and drag me across the tiles and past the loungers. I don't kick out, because I'm too exhausted to fight anymore. I can barely even breathe, I've been choked so bad.

It feels crazy when Heath flicks one of the lights on, and I see the full reality of their getup. The masks are beautiful. Twisted and evil, showing two gorgeous pairs of eyes underneath. My heart leaps with joy at the craziness, and I'm smiling as the pair of them pull their masks off.

My two stunning assailants still have a glint of malice in their eyes.

"What are you going to do to me?" I ask them, squirming at their feet – the kitchen floor hard against my back.

"What any *vampire* would do to their victim, curva." Heath lowers himself to the floor. "Bite. Hard."

It's my exposed tits Heath goes for first, crushing one as he clamps his mouth over the other. He isn't lying. His bite is fierce enough that I cry out, and then he sucks, hard. Josh joins him on the floor, licking up my damp cheek before his lips brush my ear.

"This proposal is exactly what you wanted, isn't it? You've been dreaming of this ever since series one."

My boyfriend bites my shoulder, sinking his teeth in before sucking as hard as Heath. Two hot mouths hurting so fucking bad – but it feels fucking amazing.

Heath finishes up on one tit and leans over me for my other, and I play with the one he's left. So sore. I've been love bitten by the vampire of my fantasies, and it makes me smile. My heart races to a different kind of tune and my mind races through all of the scenes I've watched of his over the years.

I hold his head to me, welcoming him as Polly Anna did when she finally succumbed to her true desires and let the Count have his way with her. His hand is warm on my drenched pussy. He tugs my soaked panties to the side and plays with me as Josh lowers himself – shooting me a dirty smirk as he goes. Damn, he looks so fine in Heath's posh gear. He teases my thigh with his tongue before he sinks his teeth in and takes up another round of sucking, his face close to Heath's fingers as they work at me.

It's Josh who gets me out of my dress and tears my panties down.

The floor beneath us is slippery wet, and it only adds to the sensation. Josh's mouth is savage on my thighs, and Heath trails a path of bites down my chest to my stomach. I've been a pain slut for years, used to the high that comes from torment turning to joy, but I'm not used to the clench of teeth and the beautiful tenderness of being feasted on.

I watch them kissing as they take a break, still playing with my sparking clit. I watch the Count kiss Josh like he kisses Polly Anna, and yeah, he's one hell of an actor, but there's a churn in my gut. A fresh round of butterflies.

This isn't acting. It's real.

Their desire is completely authentic when they go for each other's suit trousers and set free their magnificent cocks. I want them inside me. Both of them. I want them kissing each other as they fuck my love bitten, pain slut flesh.

"Please," I say. "Use me. My *fate* belongs to you, *Count*. I want to serve you. Both of you."

They break their kiss, and Josh smirks. "Yeah, I bet you do. What you really mean is that you want us to fuck you, you dirty little *curva*."

I arch my back against the tiles, teeth chattering in the aftermath of the pool.

"You know me too well, Josh."

"I know every inch of you, inside and out. Including your filthy mind."

"Busted," I say.

From the way his eyes lock on Heath's, I know he could be saying the same to him. The more I'm around them, the more obvious it becomes.

I'm shocked when Heath grabs Josh by the throat, with the Count's cruel expression on his vampiric face.

"Cocky boy," he says. "There is only one winner here, just like there is in Kington Springs. Ella isn't the only one who'll be tweaking the proposal tonight. We're not using the Agency now."

He shoves Josh to the floor at my side, and tears his shirt open, buttons going flying.

Oh my fucking God.

I shuffle away and raise myself for a better view, my hand snaking down between my legs as another scene of my dreams unfolds before me.

Heath bites Josh. Hard.

The Count bites my boyfriend, on his ripped chest, with as much savagery as he did me.

"Fuck!" Josh cries, but he doesn't fight. His cock is still rock solid, barbells glistening as Heath works a path down his body, biting and sucking until he reaches his thigh.

"You're going to be a bitten mess like your girlfriend," Heath tells him. "Remember this tomorrow when we're playing a different game."

He tugs Josh's shoes off and his trousers follow before he hoists Josh's legs right up to his chest. And then he ploughs his ass – shunting his massive cock right the way to the balls, the barbells taking no prisoners as they pop their way in, one after the other.

That's got to fucking hurt, real fucking bad. Josh groans through gritted teeth as the glorious Count pounds his asshole – his long dark hair, dripping wet. I'm a mute spectator, open mouthed and still drenched myself, and I don't know what to do other than play with my pussy.

Heath clicks his fingers to bring me out of my daze.

"Clean me," he says, and pulls his cock free.

I scrabble towards him, not giving a fuck for anything but obeying his command. It's his tone. His energy. His character.

He takes my hair as I clean his dirty cock, sucking him with whimpers.

"Good curva."

Then he plunges right back into Josh's ass again, my face up close to the action.

It's fucking beautiful.

Fucking, cleaning, biting. It's a whirlwind. Teeth, cock and fingers as Heath manoeuvres me at his whim and invades my pussy all the way to the knuckles.

"Suck your boyfriend as I come," Heath says, and again, I do as instructed without hesitation.

I take Josh's veined cock in my mouth, working him as best I can while Heath ravages his asshole.

I'm so proud of myself when they come in sync.

So proud as I swallow every last spurt of my boyfriend's hot cum.

I collapse on the floor, running my fingers over my love bites as I revel in the aftermath.

But it's not over yet. That's clear in both of the guys' dirty smiles as they look at me.

"Your ass next, *Polly Anna*," Heath says, and I grin with horny glee.

I raise my knees to my bruising tits gladly.

"Bite her," Heath says, working his cock again.

I groan like the slut I truly am when Josh bites down on my pussy.

And I moan for more when his teeth land on my clit.

"Harder," Heath says, and fuck, it takes my all not to scream as Josh obeys, biting down hard and sucking.

My whole body is burning, buzzing – subspace here I come.

"I'm ready," Heath says. "Hold her legs back."

Josh gives my sore clit a flick with his piercing before doing what Heath says.

"Ready for your fate, sweet curva?"

The Count's cock is rock hard, barbells glinting slick as he slips the devil mask back on and lines up his fat cock head at my asshole.

"Take me," is all I can say.

My *fate* belongs to the Count tonight.

Just like I always dreamt of.

ten

Good job last night's proposal was pretty early on this week, since these love bites are going to take a fair few days to disappear. I'm like a splotched canvas, covered in purple bruises and the unmistakable imprints of teeth marks, and I can't help but poking the wounds as a reminder of just how painful they are.

I don't call myself a pain slut for nothing, after all.

I really didn't expect Josh to be a splotched canvas too after last night's escapades, but it suits him. Everything always does.

I could get used to living like this – holed up in a sunny villa with an icon, playing filthy games every night and regaling in fun, food and hours full of chatter every day. I'm loving every single minute of it.

I'm grinning all the way through breakfast, happy with the joys of the world as I cast glances my wounded boyfriend's way. He's playful as he smiles back at me. We're definitely both feeling the vibe.

"At least you can't say you're the only one who got a night with the infamous *Count*," he says. "I got caught in the crossfire."

"You hardly pissed on my parade." My grin gets brighter. "It was brilliant. Absolutely amazing."

I'm not lying. It was absolutely fucking amazing. I'll remember that night for the rest of my life, and maybe someday I'll be lucky enough to get a re-run. I'm not pushing my luck just yet, though.

Heath isn't dressed anything like the Count this morning. He's in black shorts and a vest top, and his glorious hair is swept up into a ponytail, ready for action. Josh keeps looking at him, with a competitive tone to his smirk.

"I'm gonna kick your gorgeous ass, you know that, Heathy baby? Call it an exchange for what you did to mine last night."

Heath takes a bite of buttered toast. "You'd have to kick my ass seriously hard to make up for what I did to yours last night."

Yeah, he would. Josh was legit bleeding when Heath was done with him. Turns out that water from the swimming pool wasn't a sufficient enough lube to cope with Heath's cock assault. It's not that often I've seen Josh bleed, so Heath really did give him a good battering.

I love the way it's fuelling the fire between them today.

Who is going to be top dog on the squash court? I can't wait to be a spectator and find out. I only wish I had some pompoms.

The tension ramps up further between them as we head out to the loungers to let our breakfast settle. It's like a barometer rising with the pressure as the testosterone builds. Both guys keep jibing each other as to who is going to come out top dog, and I get the feeling this *match* has been a long time coming. I don't interject or change the topic, just soak it up and bask in the pleasure. It was me who got the full attention of a reward day yesterday, and now it's Josh's turn. I bet they'll be playing squash for hours today, neither of them willing to call it quits until they're crowned winner.

Josh sure won't ever call it quits, I know that much. Not if he's behind on the scoreboard.

It's such a shame I haven't got access to my phone, as I'd love to capture some pictures. My two sweaty loverboys battling for victory. I'd have loved pictures of the suited pair in Venetian masks last night too, and the Count all dressed up for my series preview. Damn it.

It's been a few days now, and my fingers feel fidgety at the lack of the constant accessory. I can't remember being without my phone for this long in years. My parents never confiscated it or anything like that, and my ex, Connor and I practically lived on video call when we weren't in the same room together. We even had a video call open when we were sleeping in different bedrooms. Cringe, but true. I keep instinctively reaching for my current companion of a device, but it's not there. It shows just how plugged in at the mains I am constantly. Scrolling, checking messages, watching stupid videos. Here there is nothing but me, Josh and Heath.

My fidgety fingers can get stuffed. This is so much better.

"Ready for a game, Josh?" Heath says, finally.

"Always," Josh replies. "Thought you'd never get round to asking."

Heath looks at me. "How about you, curva? Are you staying in the sun or coming along to observe our challenge?"

The streaming sun feels so nice against my bruised skin on the lounger, and the pool looks so tempting for another dip, but I can't miss out on the competition.

"Definitely coming. I might be coming at the sight of you, too. It'll be hotter than the sun out here."

"Coming over a game of squash?" Josh laughs. "Your pussy never stops aching, does it?"

"No, dumbass. Over a game of *you* playing squash. There's quite a difference. And no, my pussy never stops aching, you're right." Aching for Josh more than anything. He looks gorgeous, so ripped in his tight black vest top and shorts.

I've already been wondering about tonight's envelope and what the proposal could involve. From being a fisted puppet to a food platter to a vampire chase victim, I really have no idea. Heath could definitely surprise me. He surprises me in every other way. Including with his villa.

It's like a forbidden kingdom when he opens a side door off from the guest room hallway to reveal a set of slate steps going down.

"Ladies first," Heath says, and I'm the one who gets the first glimpse.

Fuck, it doesn't disappoint. Heath's *games room* is massive. It must be as big as the whole imprint of the villa up above, but no sunlit windows, just stark bright lights embedded in the ceiling. I scan my eyes over the place. Gym, yes – quite an impressive one. I might even hit the treadmill myself in the days to come. Pool table, check, with a whole load of space around it and tables for drinks. Dartboard. Wow, I'd love a go on that, but I'm so crap at darts that I rarely even hit the board.

And there it is. The squash court. A flash version of the one at our local gym!

The glass front will give me a fantastic view of what's happening inside, the markings on the floor plainly obvious. There's a bench, just right for spectators, so I plonk my sore butt down and prepare for the viewing. Hardly Nighttime Whispers, but hey ho, it'll be an incredible show nonetheless. Heath AND Joshua. Double whammy of awesome.

And they are both mine.

I have to give my mind a kicking. Because despite what the butterflies keep telling me, they aren't both mine at all. Heath is a client. Nothing more. He's no more to us than any of our other clients, and never will be. Any of them could offer us a trip overseas, just fine, and we could accept it, just fine. This is fine. Normal.

Except it's not.

Heath isn't a regular client... and it's about much more than Nighttime Whispers.

I see the way they smile at each other as Heath hands Josh a racquet from a locker at the far end of the court. The affectionate cheekiness makes me ache inside. I know Heath is a major celebrity, and I know he's almost always got his guard up, but with Josh there is no guard there at all. He's just himself.

And slowly but surely, he's beginning to be nothing more than himself around me, too.

"Ready to get your ass kicked?" he asks as Josh spins his racquet in his hand.

"Ready to kick your ass. You wait."

"May the best man win."

Josh laughs. "Don't put it like that, Heath, or you might have to nail it by default."

"Don't be mushy, please. I'll feel worse for thrashing you." Heath pats Josh's ass with his racquet, but the blush of his cheeks shows just how much he's loving it.

"Go, guys!" I shout as they open the glass door to the court, and Josh tuts at me.

"You're supposed to be on Team Joshua, Ells. I'm the one who's your boyfriend, remember? You need a *'go, Josh'* placard, not a penchant for the great *Count*, out to kick my ass on the squash court."

"And the *Count* is also my client who owns the villa. I'll be a double cheerleader. Why choose, right? I want you both hot and sweaty and out to win the crown, not just one of you."

"I'm not just out to win the crown," Josh says. "I'm going to take it, stick it on my head and wear it all night long."

"You reckon?" Heath says, as he steps inside. "Let's see."

The door closes behind them, and my heart races at the beginning of what's going to be such an amazing game. Heath Mason against my boyfriend. Jeez. It's another crazy experience that people would die for.

Oh my fucking God, how the guys go for it on that court –

even through the warmup. The barometer of tension is off the scale, way more intense than it was on the loungers earlier. Sweat is dripping within minutes, despite the fact that Josh hasn't even found his true bearings yet. He's still finding his feet as the pair of them dash back and forth after the ball, which is unusual. Josh normally takes the lead from the off. For a player who usually practices solo, Heath can clearly knock it out of the park. Which is quite an apt analogy really, considering that Heath usually practices solo on a lot of fronts, not just sports related…

He definitely manages to knock it out of the park on those.

They both get in position after their warmup, Josh ready to serve first in game number one, and I may have thought they were going for it in the warmup, but I'd underestimated them. The lunges are insane, the leaps beyond this world, and the way they stride and jostle across the court gives me butterflies all the way down to my toes.

Now. Here. In Heath's man cave basement-cum-sports-hall, these two could just be two hot guys from a normal walk of life playing a match together. Heath's icon status and Josh being a hooker means nothing. They are just two men giving their all to a squash match.

The way they grin at each other between rounds makes the butterflies ramp up even harder.

The competition is definitely raging, but so is the lust.

And more.

There is more than testosterone, lust and competition at play on the court.

The guys flash me smiles and waves between rounds, but their hearts aren't with me right now. They are all for each other.

I like that.

Scrap that. I *love* the way they are so consumed with each other. Even though I'm out of the spotlight. I don't care.

I probably love it a little too much, in fact.

It gives me weird ideas about how things could be on the outside world. If we were just regular people in London, and Josh was free to grab his sports kit and head out for a game of squash with Heath at a local gym. Maybe they'd go for a bite to eat after. Maybe some drinks. Maybe I'd join them. We could hang out until we decided whose place we were going home to.

Because that would happen.

We'd always go home together…

I banish the thought, because it can't be. It will never be. Heath is a client. A famous client. And we are just paid whores out to entertain him for a week between stints of filming.

So why are both my heart and gut telling me otherwise? Tempting me with a crazy dream?

My attention gets tugged back to the court when Josh lets out an especially loud cheer at a victory. I've lost track of the scorecard, but they haven't. Josh is two points up.

It only spurs Heath on.

They take a break, absolutely drenched in sweat as they glug some water on the bench with me. Fuck, I'd love some action with them like this, but the testosterone is nowhere near my pussy when they towel the sweat from their brows. They get set to jump right back in there.

"You're really fucking good," Josh says to Heath.

"You sound really fucking surprised."

Josh shrugs. "Maybe I am."

"Maybe I'll surprise you some more. First to ten?"

"Yeah, let's do it."

I'm surprised they make it to ten, honestly. Their muscles are going to be aching like fucking hell tomorrow after the workout they've been doing in there.

You couldn't make it up when they get to nine all and it comes down to the final play.

I can barely look, because it's too intense for fucking words.

Whoever comes out on top is going to be singing it from the rooftops.

I'm open mouthed when it's Heath that steals the victory, because WTF?? Something subconscious in me always assumes Josh is going to win, I guess. He's built to be a winner in any circumstance, and with sport he takes it so seriously.

My boyfriend is shaking his head when they step out of there, but there is no animosity, just admiration on his face as he stares at the man before him.

"You slayed it," he says. "Fucking hell, Heath, if Nighttime Whispers dries up, take up squash. You're like a bloody pro."

"Thanks."

That one simple word is all Heath has to say about his glory. No gloating, like I figured there would be. No yelling to the rafters and claiming to be the dog's bollocks. Just a handshake and a *really enjoyed that, honestly, you rocked it.*

From an outsider's point of view, you'd think this was Heath's reward, not Josh's.

That makes me feel kinda sad.

Heath Mason enjoying a squash game this much – as though it's an anomaly of daily life.

Guess it is, though, for a man like him.

We're back up in the kitchen when Heath presents the next proposal envelope. He looks almost sheepish as I take it from him, holding up his hands.

"This is a weird one, ok? Just something I wanted. Something I've been missing, for a long, long time." He looks between me and Josh. "I figured that today might only reinforce it, and I was right. It did."

Once again, I'm full speed as I tear the proposal from the envelope.

Whatever Heath has been missing, we're going to give it to him.

eleven

WEDNESDAY

I've always been a loner, and one of my regrets in life is not indulging in the reckless, freestyle fun of university students trashed on wine.
Indulging in fun and flirting, and drunken games.
I would like you to indulge me, and help me gain a taste of what it would have been like.
Truth or dare, spin the bottle, strip poker, and would-you-rather games. Dirty, and fun. Who will win some of those, Joshua? I hope you are still in competition mode.
Be my college buddies tonight, sweet curvas. Reveal your secrets, and share in mine.
Let's crack open the wine and have some fun.

Proposal duration – 4 hours-ish!
Reward – a wine tasting experience at one of the region's finest vineyards

I read the proposal through for a second time, grinning in disbelief, because it wasn't what I was expecting at all. I was expecting some hardcore BDSM, or a game of *who can take it?* Not flirty, dirty games as we glug on wine.

An evening of *college fun* sounds amazing, and nothing I ever actually got the chance to indulge in either. I didn't go to university. I was always too busy supporting Connor's music dreams to plan out a career for myself. I was certain he'd make it – and yes, despite being an absolute asshole, he did make it. I was sure as fuck I'd be by his side when he did hit the limelight – but no, I wasn't.

Too bad.

When I was holed up in my shitty bedsit, crying over my loss with barely twenty quid in my bank account, it felt as though my whole life was in ashes.

Oh, how I was wrong.

Funny how life works in mysterious ways.

I sure as fuck never thought I'd be here, with the true love of my life and Heath Mason, my onscreen idol, playing *college games*.

"Do you like the sound of that proposal?" Heath asks me. "Not quite up to the *hardcorer* level you're used to, I imagine."

"I love the sound of the proposal," I tell him, and opt for honesty before we've even started on truth or dare. "I don't really have the university scenario to draw on, but I'll do my best. It was always me and my ex hanging out together, and sure, I got trashed a few times and had some filthy fun in threesomes and foursomes and stuff, but I never got the chance for this kind of thing." I look at Josh, picturing him and his best friend Tiffany together, and the raucous laughter through the party games they must have shared over the years.

I want a taste of that, too...

With Heath, as well as my boyfriend.

"How about you, Josh?" Heath asks him. "Does the proposal tickle your fancy?"

"I'm definitely still in competition mode, so hell yeah, it tickles my fancy. I'm going to kick your ass at whatever games we play, Heathy baby, don't worry about that."

"We'll see."

"Yes, we will."

I want to start with the truth or dares from the off, but the guys insist it's time for dinner first. Wine will knock us out too early on an empty stomach, Heath assures me.

Josh is chef this evening and starts up making one of his mum's hearty recipes. A delicious cottage pie with roasted veg. I love having it at her place, and I love Josh's version, too.

"Smells incredible," Heath says, but Josh holds up a hand when our client attempts to check it out in the kitchen area.

"Keep your nosey arse out of here, please. I want you to savour the full surprise when it hits your plate."

"I'm going to be using my nosey *arse* all night, Josh. Better get used to it. And plenty of *full surprises* will be heading your way, as well as mine."

I have a feeling there will indeed be plenty of surprises this evening. Something feels… strange.

Human.

Fuck it, I can't help starting up with the questions. Truth or dare, and client confidentiality and all that stuff can get fucked for once.

"Do you ever have people cook for you? Chefs on call, that kind of thing?" I ask Heath as he takes a seat beside me at the breakfast bar.

"Not for years, besides the occasional takeaway delivery. I'm quite the lone wolf. Luckily, I'm a good enough chef to serve myself."

"You're a great chef. Your cooking rocks."

Heath gives me such a beautiful smile. "It's nice to be able to share my talents with other people's plates."

My blabbermouth opens before my brain kicks in.

"Maybe our proposals could be longer when we are back in London together? We could have proposal days as well as nights. Hang out like we do here…"

Heath nods, but looks towards the setting sun through the window, not at me. He seems, reserved? Distracted? I dunno.

"I'd like that," he says. "I'd like that a lot."

So would I. And Josh would. I know it.

I get a pang for Heath, which is bizarre given that he's not the kind of man I'd ever figured I'd get a pang of sympathy for. He shouldn't need to pay for any kind of company whatsoever. People would be flocking around him, all day and all night long, if he wanted them there.

"I was always a bit of a lone wolf, it's not a recent development," Heath tells me. "Apart from when the high of the spotlight first hit. I was one of the goth kids in the shadows at school. A weirdo on the outskirts."

"Me, too. Until I met Connor."

"Connor? Your ex, right?"

"Yes, my ex."

I don't want to tell Heath how Connor finally shot to fame with a viral song about a hooker girlfriend who broke his heart. I can't stand the bloody song. That bullshit was still all over social media when we flew out here. One good thing about not having my phone is not seeing posts about that shitty song everywhere I look.

"How long were you together?" Heath asks.

"Too long. Way, way, way too long. He's a real piece of shit."

Heath grins. "Most people say that about their exes, I find."

Josh heads to the fridge and takes out a bottle of wine. He presents it to us along with three glasses, a towel over his shoulder as he maintains his chef role.

"My ex tore my heart to shreds and then laughed about it," he says. "She was a jackass with a decent ass. Not as good as Ella's though."

"Magpie, yes?" Heath says.

"Yeah. I'm actually pleased she fucked me over. If she hadn't, I wouldn't have met Ella."

I grin as he pours our wine.

"Same," I tell him. "I'm glad Connor fucked me over, too. Or I wouldn't have met you." I take my glass and hold it up to Heath. "Or you."

Heath raises his glass back at me. "I'm glad to be included in that statement. I'm sure plenty of your other clients would feel the same. We should send him a thank you card. He gave us a treasure."

The walls between client and lover are crumbling by the day, I can feel it, and I can see it in Heath's eyes. Not just in the way he looks at Josh, either. It's spreading further than that. Blossoming like a rose in bloom between me and him as well. That goes both ways. My walls are crumbling, too. Heath is becoming far more to me than Heath Mason the superstar could ever be...

My thoughts are interrupted by Josh presenting the prized cottage pie on the worktop – a steaming tray of perfection. The potatoes have browned around the edges of the dish just right.

"This is really something," Heath says, and his stare lingers on Josh.

Josh meets his eyes with one of the meaningful looks of his that make me tingle. He raises his wine glass.

"Yes, it is. Cheers."

We all give a *cheers* and begin our evening as Josh serves up our dinner. The questions turn back into regular conversation as we all eat together at the dining table, the guys recounting the intensity of their squash matches earlier. They laugh, they talk tactics. They talk like lovers. And I listen. I love listening to both of their voices as I munch on cottage pie and roasted veg.

And all the while, the wine flows.

I love the headiness as one bottle follows the other. I adore the way the sun begins to set through the window, so stunningly.

I'm the one who clears the dinner plates away, waving off the guys' offer of help so they can carry on talking squash tactics. I watch them as I load the dishwasher, trying to imagine this being London instead of here, and Heath being at our place, instead of his. How amazing it would be.

"Where are we having our games night?" I ask when I return, and Heath points towards the living room.

"Head on through and make yourselves comfy. I'll stock us up on wine. We'll be needing it."

Josh and I saunter towards the lounge with our glasses in our hands. I find I'm looking up at him, examining his expression.

"What?" he asks with a smirk.

"You have a real thing for him, don't you? Like a *real* real thing."

Josh pulls me in and kisses my cheek.

"That's a truth or dare question, I'd say. Quit it. The proposal hasn't started yet."

"What if he asks? In truth or dare, I mean. What if Heath asks what your feelings are towards him?"

We reach the living room and Josh moves the coffee table so it's closer to the corner sofa. Easy access for all three of us.

"I'm not sure what I'll say," he replies. "What is there to say? He's a great client. I love our time together."

"That's not the truth and you know it."

Josh takes a seat, and pats the cushion beside him.

"Guess I'd better keep taking dares, then. And it *is* the truth. He is a great client and I do love our time together."

Do you love HIM?

Part of me wants to ask him that question myself, truth or dare be damned. I've had my suspicions, but it's becoming so obvious now – emotions simmering as the days move on. And it's boiling fast.

How the fuck are we going to be feeling by the time we have to take a flight home?

That's a question I don't want to be thinking about.

Heath has four bottles of wine with him when he joins us. I'm in the corner seat, and he flops down on my right side once he's put the bottles on the table. His eyes are mischievous and alive, as though this really is a party game night. And it needs to be. It's his proposal after all.

"We've got too many bottles to go before a spin the bottle just yet," he laughs. "So, what do we do first? Any suggestions?"

"*Would you rather?*" I say. "I love that game."

"Sounds good. Rock, paper, scissors for who goes first?"

Josh wins, as bloody usual. He whacks my scissor fingers with his fist.

He takes a swig of wine while he ponders his question, as though he's contemplating life itself.

"Heath… would you rather take it up the ass in public, or never be an actor again?"

Ouch. That's a deep one. I raise my eyebrows at him.

"What?" Josh asks. "This is an authentic games night, right? Let's hit it right from the off."

I look at Heath, who leans back against the sofa cushions, his fingers knitted together across his chest.

"What do you mean when you say public, exactly?"

"I mean, you get caught by the paparazzi, being fucked in the ass by a hot stud in a back alley."

Heath winces. "I wouldn't particularly want videos of my ass being savaged popping up all over the internet. Hot stud or not."

"Exactly, genius." Josh laughs. "That's the fucking point. Would you rather that than give up your career? What's it gonna be? Career success or taking a viral slammer online?"

"I love my career," Heath says. "It's extremely important to me."

"I know."

"But so is staying private."

"Yes, I know." Josh fake sighs. "Jesus, Heath, good job you didn't get to play this college buddy shit for real, or you'd still be there now. It's supposed to be quickfire."

Heath holds up his hands.

"Fine. Career. I'd give up my career."

Josh widens his eyes. "Whoa. Ok."

Heath narrows his. "Are you really that surprised?"

The tension has already ramped – my gaze flicking between the pair of them with their locked stares.

"It's alright to take it up the ass, Heath. It's no crime."

"I know that, Josh. This isn't a counselling session. I just wouldn't want my ass cheeks spread all over social media, thanks."

"Social media would," I laugh, trying to interject. "People would go crazy for it."

"I'm plenty in the spotlight as it is," he tells me. "I don't want people fawning over my ravaged asshole. They fawn over my ass plenty enough."

"Fine," Josh says. "Career it is. Your go."

Heath looks between the two of us.

"Ella… would you rather find Josh in bed with your ex, or in bed with your mum?"

My eyes open wide in horror, even at the thought.

"Jesus, Heath! My ex, definitely. It would at least be vaguely hot. I just hope Connor's ass would get torn to utter shit by the barbells."

"And would you forgive him for it?"

I shake my head. "Forgive Josh? No! No way in hell. Connor is a smarmy tosser and can talk a good game, but any kind of betrayal like that would have me out of the door. For good."

"Good job I won't be fucking your ex then, isn't it?" Josh squeezes my knee. "He's not my type anyway."

"You've seen him?" Heath asks.

"I've had the unfortunate experience of meeting him. Multiple times. Ella wasn't lying when she said he's a jackass. I wouldn't go within a mile of his ass with a bargepole."

My turn for the *would you rather* question.

I go for Josh, and fuck it. I swig back a whole glass of wine before I let rip. Let's get this party fucking started.

"Would you rather give up your entire client base, or… give up Heath?"

Fuck, I regret the question as soon as I've said it. Josh gives me fucking evils, in disbelief as he stares at me.

That touched deep.

He switches his demeanour in seconds, playing it casual, but I know how hard I've jabbed.

"Depends on how much he was paying." Josh laughs as he looks at Heath. "Would you outbid the rest of my client base if it came to it, Heathy baby?"

Heath doesn't laugh.

"Yes."

Josh carries on with the tomfoolery regardless.

"They pay me pretty well."

"I don't give a fuck. I'd pay you better."

"In that case, I'd take you over them regardless. Pay rise!" Josh rubs his hands together.

I could thump him in the ribs for evading the question like that, because that's not what I was asking, and he knows it. He knows what I wanted to hear – even if curiosity does kill the cat.

Josh's turn next. I see the dark humour in his eyes as they land on mine.

"Tit for tat. Ella, would you rather give up your entire client base, or give up Heath?"

Shit.

It's not as easy a question as I figured it would be.

Instinct has my mind whirring through all of the clients I've formed dirty bonds with since taking up my position at the Agency. From *Daddy* to the masked CNC freak who chases me through cowsheds, to the utterly crazy savagery of the Agency *founders* and the blissful subspace that comes from their insane rounds of sadism…

Mr Monthly and our messy fun whenever I'm on my period. My roleplay clients… the incredible humiliation scenes where I get to be a trashy piece of meat for hours on end and love it.

The thought of giving up all of that gives me a thump in the guts far harder than the thump in the ribs I wanted to give Josh. And I get it. From the intensity in his eyes, I get it.

He felt the same way… it's not an easy call.

So, I use the same fucking copout he did.

I turn to Heath with a beaming smile.

"Would you outbid the rest of my clients if it came to it, *Heathy baby*? Or is that privilege reserved for Josh?"

"Of course I would," Heath answers.

"In that case, the answer is obvious. It's a yes from me."

Heath puts a hand on his heart. There is a steely depth to his stare, despite the fact he's smiling.

"Well, I am flattered. If I gave you a pay rise, you'd opt for my company over any other's. What a beautiful thing to hear. Such adoration."

He laughs, but he's not being genuine. He's as fake as we are.

Alarm bells go off in my head, because as proposals go, we're failing bad at this one. This isn't college humour and games, this is… personal.

"You should be flattered," Josh says. "I have some incredible clients I'd have to give up."

"Ditto," I say, but Heath brushes it aside.

"I'm sure you do, and good job this is a *would you rather* rather than a *will you have to*. I'm happy to share."

Is he, though? Really?

THE NAUGHTY WEEK

"Strip poker time!" I say. "Come on, I want to see you two with your cocks out. I'm too horny for much more *would you rather*."

The guys buy into it, and Heath takes out a poker set from a drawer underneath the coffee table. I breathe a sigh of relief as he sets us up, and I paste on a smile – happy to be back in the familiar turf of performing and nudity.

The guys give an excellent strip show, one piece of clothing at a time, and they may have been competing at squash and kicking ass all day, but I definitely top the leaderboard on this one.

I make it filthy. Really fucking filthy. Splaying my pussy to show off the treasure when the game has me taking my panties off. The last item to play for…

"I'm going to make such a mess of your sofa," I say to Heath. "I'm so fucking wet."

"Good," he replies, and tops up my wine glass. *Again.* "So, how about truth or dare?"

He rises to straddle me and rubs his swollen shaft against my slit.

"How could I resist? Go for it," I say. "Truth."

"Tell me then, *Holly*. What does your favourite client make you do for them? Excluding me, of course."

I know the answer in a heartbeat. My eyes are on Heath's as I answer.

"A client known as *Daddy*. He makes me call him Daddy while I pretend to be his naughty little girl all through the night."

Heath keeps rubbing his cock against my slit.

"Tell me more."

It feels so dirty to tell Heath how I perform for my client. How I'm the daughter he catches fucking her boyfriend, and how badly he punishes me for it. How he tells me that *Daddy* is the only one allowed to do those things to me, and how he washes me clean after I've been *soiled*. How he makes me feel like a naughty little bitch when I'm over his knee and taking a spanking.

And how wonderfully wrong it feels when he dumps me in a bathtub and puts the shower on cold, while he 'cleans' my fake boyfriend's dirty cum out of me...

"He fucks you with a flannel?" Heath says, and I nod.

"Yeah. Drenched in ice cold water and wrapped over his fingers. And he makes me gargle warm water straight from the shower hose... to get the taste of cock out of my mouth. He's so good with the name calling as well. His roleplay skills are off the chart." I pause. "I get so much morning after syndrome from him... honestly. I begin to believe I'm that dirty little college girl for real."

"Morning after syndrome?"

"It's a term we use at the Agency," Josh explains, with his hard cock in his hand. "It's when the fantasy bleeds over into real life. Becomes kind of emotional. It's fleeting. Usually."

"How about me?" Heath asks. "Do I ever give you *morning after syndrome?*"

I nod. "Every. Single. Time."

Josh grabs one of my tits, squeezing hard. "You've given him a truth for free. He owes us one now."

Heath's cock is so close to my pussy. I want him inside me so fucking bad.

"Truth or dare," my boyfriend says to Heath.

"Truth," Heath replies, still working his swollen cock head against my clit.

"Would you *want* to give her morning after syndrome? What is it, Heath? Do you sink back into the shadows when Ella leaves, without a second thought about her... or do you *want* it to hurt her to leave you?"

This is such a fucked up twist.

Call it a whole load of wine, and drunken mouths and swollen cocks, but Josh has a different edge to his voice now. Digging.

"That's not a fair question," Heath replies. "I'll switch to dare."

Josh takes a fistful of his hair, pressing his mouth right up to

Heath's ear – and I see the dominant side of my boyfriend. One that makes my pulse race.

"No switching, Heath. Answer the question. Do you want my girlfriend to be hurting when she has to leave you? Do you want her to pine for you between sessions?"

"I wouldn't want to hurt Ella, Josh. Not emotionally."

"That's not what I'm asking." He angles Heath's face down, so his eyes are locked on mine. "Look at her, baby, and tell me. Do you want my girlfriend to be hurting when she leaves you? Do you want her to need you so fucking bad, it makes her ache?"

I hitch up, coaxing Heath's cock inside me. *Please.*

Josh's words are fucked up, but hot.

"I'll want Ella to be baring my marks when you fly away," Heath says. "I certainly want to make our proposals fucking memorable. That's not in question."

"Fuck you, Heath, just answer the real question. Fuck her cunt, and tell me the truth."

One pop of a barbell, and I moan for him. I know what I want the answer to be…

Two, and I wince, my pussy so desperate, it's screaming.

"Answer the fucking question, Heath," Josh says again. "You opted for truth, so give it to me. Do you want my girlfriend to be aching after you? Missing you? Crazy with the need to see you again once you say goodbye?"

A pause. So heated, it fucking burns.

"SAY IT!" Josh snaps. "Cut the crap, Heath, and just fucking say it!"

"You already know the fucking answer," Heath says, and slams all four of the other barbells in, balls deep in my pussy as I yelp. "Yes, I want her to fucking miss me. I want to give her *morning after syndrome*, I want to drive her fucking crazy, and you know it. You've known it since you very first brought her along to my place and admitted she was your fucking girlfriend while my cock was buried deep."

Heath's eyes are so deep and savage on Josh's.

"You can give me a truth yourself now, Josh baby. It's what *you* wanted, isn't it? From the moment you brought her along, you wanted me to be aching too. That's why you told me she was your girlfriend. You knew it would change the game."

Heath fucks me as I moan, my tits bobbing as the two men above me battle out in a stare – just as severe in tension as they were on the court earlier.

"Yes, I knew it would change the game," my boyfriend admits.

"And how about you? Do you ever suffer with *morning after syndrome* when you leave my place, or do you just whistle as you walk away?"

Josh tugs on Heath's hair, running his tongue up my idol's cheek.

"I had morning after syndrome from the very first moment I met you, Heath. I was already aching before I walked away."

Jesus Christ, how they kiss.

It's fucking magical.

Tongues twisting, breaths ragged with grunts and groans as the two men devour each other. It was an explosion of magnitude all set to unleash. A truth ready to boom into the air.

And now it has, it won't be forgotten. Drunken games night aside, it may be buried under *banter*, but it's there now. The veil has been ripped away.

"I've got a dare now for you both now," I moan up at them, Heath's cock grating at just the right angle. "Be brave boys and double up in my cunt with no rubbers or lube."

That's a fucking dare alright. One false move and their piercings could snag on each other's. Ouch. Blood, sweat and stinging cocks.

THE NAUGHTY WEEK

"Dare accepted," Josh says. "Unless Heath is going to be a pussy about it."

Josh pulls away from Heath and reclines on the sofa beside me, working his giant pierced cock in his hand.

Heath tears his dick out of me in one, and the pair of them haul me onto Josh's cock, my cunt sucking him in like a hungry mouth. *A hungry mouth that is hungry for two...*

"I'm not a pussy, Josh. I *want* pussy."

"From competition to teamwork," Josh says as Heath lines up. "Better be careful. If we tangle piercings, we'll be a mess."

"Good job we know each other so well then, isn't it?" Heath says, watching Josh's dick pumping into me. "Let's fuck your girlfriend's cunt on the same fucking pitch."

Josh pulls out so both men can work their cocks together, and I smile at the ceiling, drunk – heady and waiting. They normally use rubbers for two in one.

Taking two is going to hurt... especially without a warmup.

My cunt has to strain like fuck to take them both at once. Their cocks are so in sync that there is no wiggle room, nothing but one solid double pole that forces its way inside, and then uses me – with deep, long thrusts that have me moaning like the slut I am.

Josh and Heath are two teammates working in perfect union as they savage my pussy, and they are still in perfect union as they reach the crest – Heath striking a delight of a chord for my benefit, with his thumb on my clit.

Excellent work, partners.

We are all on the same team as we come together, my tits bobbing as I groan and swallow them up, crazy for deep, deep, deep, fucking DEEPER!

Heaven is a place on Earth.

It's in a villa in France, on a weeklong vacation.

The guys are very careful in the aftermath, pulling out slowly to check out their cum slick cocks. Phew. They haven't tangled. No piercings snagged.

"Great work," I say as I catch my breath. "Top marks for that dare. You got me good."

Heath smiles down at me, with a dirty sparkle in his eye.

"About what you shared earlier..." he says. "About a man you call *Daddy*..."

I lick my lips. "What about him?"

He spreads my thighs, checking out my cum dripping pussy.

"You said he uses a flannel to clean you out when you've been a naughty girl... in freezing cold water..."

"Yes, he does."

Heath tips his head towards the doorway.

"I've got another suggestion for a party game," he says. "*Show not tell.*"

Josh nips at my shoulder.

"Fuck, yeah. You'd better get your ass in that shower for Heathy baby," my boyfriend tells me. "I think our client wants to try out *fatherhood*."

"Gladly," I giggle, and let Heath help me to my feet.

The energy has changed and lightened by the time we each take another glass of wine with a *cheers*, and Heath is back to our *client* again. All fun and games, and kinky proposals.

But the truth is out there now. Its face has been unveiled in the room.

Morning after syndrome has nothing on how Josh and I feel about *Heathy baby*.

Leaving him behind always hurts.

And it's only going to get worse.

twelve

*H*eath is seriously bloody good when it comes to disguises. I barely recognise him when he appears from the dressing room in his baseball cap and sunglasses. His hair is twisted up so tightly, you can't see so much as a glimpse of it, and his glasses block out any hint of his iconic eyes. There is no hint as to the shape of his brows, his shades are so big, and he's dressed in a faded black t-shirt and bland grey shorts. Boring. Safe. Just a tourist set to blend into the background.

He told us to tone it down ourselves, so as not to draw any attention, hence I've opted for a basic cami dress and slathered myself in suntan lotion, rather than makeup. It feels odd to be bare faced, without fake lashes or scarlet lipstick on when I'm heading out for the day. Hell, I even wore eyeliner to the supermarket I worked at.

Josh looks different today, too – his hair styled flat and dull, the purple streak hidden under a blue baseball cap. He's wearing one of Heath's outfits – a beige vest top and some cutoff jeans.

We look so unlike our usual weirdo selves, I could almost laugh.

This isn't the red-carpet style glamour I'd ever have expected around a superstar like Heath Mason. I used to imagine plenty of red-carpet encounters with him when I was fangirling through Nighttime Whispers over the years, revelling in my imagination and doing Connor's head in. Yet, when the cab pulls up to the villa, set to take us to our vineyard destination, I find those previous fantasies don't mean shit, not in the slightest. I don't need glamour around Heath. The simplicity of him being him in a stupid disguise is way more than enough to have me grinning my head off – over the moon, in fact.

"I've chosen somewhere deluxe for us," he tells me and Josh in the back seat, as though we would be expecting anything less for our *reward*. "They do gorgeous whites, still and sparkling."

"That's for me, isn't it?" I nudge his elbow. "You know I'm a sucker for sparkling. You prefer red."

He holds his hands up. "Guilty as charged. But this is your treat, not mine."

I lower my glasses far enough to shoot him a side eye. "Have you ever had this treat yourself? Have you been on many tours? Luxury red grapes and wine tasting?"

He looks ahead, through the windscreen.

"Once. Ages ago. It was good. Not the kind of thing you have to go on weekly."

Things have a different feel to them after truth or dare last night. Despite wiping the depths aside with more filth, fun and games, and a load more frolicking, the veil has been ripped away – and it's irreversible. I've seen much further into Heath Mason's guarded soul.

Lone wolf.

That may be what Heath calls himself, and he's introverted, yeah definitely, but a loner? I'd say he's more *lonely* than he'd care to admit.

I get a lurch at the memory of some of the admissions last night. The way he looked at me as he coughed up some of his true feelings and Josh burst out his in response.

I'd love to ask Heath more questions, about what he wants, what he likes, what he'd really be doing if he didn't feel so handi-

THE NAUGHTY WEEK

capped by the spotlight and paparazzi. Would he be visiting more vineyards and going on more excursions if we were here with him on a more permanent basis? Would he one day feel comfortable ditching the cap and the shades, just a little bit at a time?

It's only when Josh clears his throat to get my attention that I realise how intently I'm staring at Heath while he stares out at the road ahead.

Awkward.

I give a running commentary on the view outside and how amazing everything is. Fantastic streets and buildings, and views of the beach before we go inland and climb up towards fields of green.

"Here we are," Heath says when the driver pulls up to the vineyard entrance.

I get out of the car and admire the huge rows of grape vines stretching up onto the hills above us, basking in the beautiful sunlight. There must be millions of juicy wine grapes up there. Absolutely millions.

Josh takes my hand as we head for the reception and Heath steps up to the counter.

"We're here for the tour," he tells the receptionist, and his voice has changed. His tone is lower, and it sounds weird for him, but the receptionist doesn't notice, which figures. He is an actor, after all.

"Mr Christoff, yes?"

Heath nods, giving a half smile, not his regular one.

"That's right."

I don't get it when he hands his credit card over. Mr Christoff, WTF?

"If you could wait out front," the receptionist says. "The driver will be with you shortly."

"Mr Christoff?" I ask Heath once we're outside.

"My PR manager," he says. "I use his card for public outings."

The jeep is with us in seconds, and Heath steps up to speak to the driver. I use the opportunity to grab Josh by the hand and pull him close.

"Do you think Heath's paranoid? A fake ID at a vineyard? Really?" I look around. "There's nobody here."

"Heath is just Heath," Josh replies with a shrug. "I guess it's been a long time since he's been allowed to be himself in the great outdoors."

"Or allowed himself to *be* himself outside *his* front door."

"Savage. Maybe you should offer him some therapy as well as your pussy," Josh says with a smirk, but I didn't mean it that way. Not at all. Savage is the last thing I want to be when it comes to Heath.

I wouldn't recognise the celebrity client who beckons us over to the jeep and opens the back door for me. He sits opposite Josh and I with his back to the driver as we ascend through the stunning rows of grapes, being educated by the tour guide enthusiastically. It's cool. Kind of. The stuff about types of grapes and how they are grown and harvested, and all of the different grand sounding names for them is interesting, but not nearly so interesting as Heath.

He's not himself here. Not at all.

His shoulders are rigid. His smile is self-conscious. Weird for the *Count* and the man I've come to know behind closed doors.

We're out of the jeep and tasting our third type of grapes when we first get the chance to be alone. The guide is on his way back to the jeep and out of earshot when Josh leans in close enough to whisper.

"Fucking hell, I'm a shit wine connoisseur," Josh says. "Honestly, these grapes all taste like grapes to me. Kudos to the people who can sniff wines and tell which of these little bad boys go into making them, because it's a skill above my level."

It's a relief to see the way Heath returns to himself at Josh's sneaky statement. He laughs Heath's actual laugh. He smiles his actual smile. And I just know his eyes are sparkling behind his glasses.

"Same," he says. "I'd like to think of myself as a wine lover, but this really puts things into perspective. I know sweet fuck all. How about you, Ella?"

I have to laugh as I pop a grape into my mouth.

"Umm... it's a great trip. I love the scenery. And I'm sure I'll love the wine, too."

"That's a no, then," Heath says. "Ella the non-wine connoisseur, just like us."

"No!" I say. "I like grapes and stuff as well."

"We should do a *do you remember* game," Josh says. "What was the grape over in that row called, Ells?"

He points to a row three over.

"Something beginning with C..." I reply. "Char... charie?"

"Fuck knows," Josh says, and there's something about the conspiracy between us that gives me the giggles. Like naughty kids on a school trip.

The driver is waiting, and we're laughing, and now we're fucked, because every time from that point, when he lets us sample the grapes while he gives us the variety history, it's going to tickle us. I just know it.

And it does.

Slowly but surely, the three of us bloom together in technicolour, despite our boring attire. We laugh, and chat, and Heath drops his fake voice. We enjoy the sun and the greenery, and munch on grape samples with giggles, and it's great. It's really fucking great, and it will get even better when it comes to the wine tasting.

I'm gagging for some samples as the next tour guide talks us through the aging and bottling process. I feign interest, and manage it a bit, because some of this stuff is cool and I really didn't expect I'd be able to answer vineyard related questions in a pub quiz anytime this lifetime, but my primary interest is on two things only. And they definitely aren't vineyard related.

The men standing at my side are far more beautiful than rows of vines could ever be. I edge closer to Heath, testing the boundaries he has with his disguise. I brush my arm against his as our tour guide is speaking, and dare to tangle my fingers in his.

He could step away from me easily. He could create distance without a word, no problem whatsoever. But he doesn't.

Heath Mason lets me take his fingers in mine as we listen to the aging process of different types of wine at the vineyard, and then he squeezes back, just a touch.

That touch is enough.

The veil reveals another peek inside.

His walls are coming down – outside as well as in. And just imagine where that could lead…

I shouldn't imagine. I should avoid any dreams or fantasies or ponderings of any sort, and Josh reminds me of that when the guide ushers us on through to the next room, and engages *Mr Christoff* with some further information on one of the wine varieties.

"Don't do it," my boyfriend whispers. "It's not fair on any of us."

"Do what?" I ask, and his eyes fix on mine.

"You know what. It won't benefit you or me, and it definitely won't benefit him. Not when we have to fuck off out of here in a few days' time and go back to normal."

Normal.

I've already lost track of what *normal* feels like, because this, right here, THIS is what feels normal now.

"Ella," Josh whispers, knowing my thoughts as well as he knows my words. "Stop it. Seriously."

I shrug. "Fine. Ok."

"Good."

He smiles, but his smile is as fake as Heath's was when we were first in the jeep earlier. He's talking sense, but he's also talking bullshit. He doesn't want to go back to *normal* any more than I do.

"Guys!" *Mr Christoff* calls, and we look over at the client who is driving us crazy. "Come, join me. Time for wine tasting."

"Can't wait!" I clap my hands. "I'm dying to see what these grapes taste like!"

I'm not lying, either. A glug of wine is exactly what I'm needing right now.

I bounce on over, with a massive smile on my face – but this time I heed Josh's words, and I don't get too close. I don't take Heath's hand.

Fair play, the wines do taste a lot different when you try them one after the other. I get the hang of sniffing them, too. I'm still debating my favourites when we arrive at the wine store at the end of the tour, so Heath makes a Heath move and takes a load of all three of them, and a whole batch of Josh's favourite, too.

We're not going to be running out of wine anytime soon, that's for certain. And it hits me in the guts there and then.

We won't be running out of wine anytime soon regardless of this new massive selection, because in just a few days it'll be a cab driving us out of Cannes, to the airport – not driving us from a vineyard back to his place.

"Time for home," Heath says as we wait for the cab back to his villa, and his words give me one of those damn lurches. I shift from foot to foot.

Home.

It's sure beginning to feel like it.

Cliché and fucked up and forbidden or not – home is where the heart is.

And my heart is here. With Heath and Josh.

thirteen

THURSDAY

I hope you enjoyed your wine tasting session today. So many glorious flavours to choose from – fragrant and distinguished.
Time to turn that on its head.
Tonight will be a tasting of an entirely different variety – other than the shade of the liquids we'll be using.
Watersports!
We'll be glugging the piss as readily as we glug the wine. I want to see the enjoyment on your faces as you taste the nectar straight from the source.
No grapes required for the brewing.
Served warm, not cold.
There is a 'bottle' I'd like to fill, though – and you can help me with that, Josh.
Get prepared for things to get very wet, very slippery, and very very fucking dirty.
Lots of drinking beforehand, as always. We want to make sure the 'wine' keeps on flowing.

Proposal duration – until the final piss before bedtime.
Reward – a night out for you in an exclusive club in Cannes. Take your chance to explore the buzz of such a vibrant location.

. . .

Josh is still putting today's wine stock up in the chiller when I read the proposal aloud. Heath couldn't wait to hand the envelope over to me, dashing through to the bedroom to grab it when we were barely back in through the door.

The proposal makes perfect sense, knowing Heath. Piss play is one of his staples back in London.

I recall the way he watched Josh and I sipping the wine samples at the vineyard, and admiring the tastes, him knowing the whole time that he'd be filling our mouths with an entirely different substance this evening.

I shoot him a dirty look as I grab a glass from the cupboard and fill it to the brim with some icy cold mineral water. I down it in one, and wipe my lips clean.

"Damn, I am seriously parched from today. Such warm weather."

Josh gives me a smirk over his shoulder, rising to his feet when he's finished putting the wine away.

"Yeah, I'm with you on that, Ells. I'm absolutely parched myself."

He downs a glass of water in one right after me, and Heath laughs, getting a glass of his own.

"Glad to hear it. That's a yes to the proposal then, is it?"

Josh smacks his lips.

"That's hardly a truth or dare style question, Heath. You know we're with you every step of the way when it comes to this kind of proposal."

"Yes, I know that, but I wasn't joking about bottle filling. I have some ideas to play out." He pauses, looking my boyfriend right in the eyes. "You know what I'm talking about, Josh."

There are unspoken words between them. A smile that conveys they are both on the same page yet again.

But I'm not. I have no idea what the fuck they are referring to.

I rest an elbow on the counter. "I'm intrigued. What or whose *bottle* will you be filling? I don't get it."

Heath taps his nose. "You'll have to wait to find out."

Josh laughs as he pours another glass of water. "Christ, Heath, your proposals are so vague compared to our other clients. They spell it out to the letter before we agree to them, listing pretty much every fucking detail. You're the only one who uses the one liners and innuendos with me. And as for Ells, she'll have no idea what you're on about."

He's not wrong.

"How do you feel about that, Ella?" Heath asks me. "Does it bother you? Would you rather I spell it out word for word? I'm sure other clients do that for you."

I wink at him. "Yeah, they do, but you don't need to bother. What can I say? You're a one off."

Heath is smiling as he tugs his cap off and lets his hair fall free.

"I'm a special client, am I?"

"Very."

He takes a glug of water from his glass, then tips his head to the side. Now his glasses are off, the full beauty of his stunning, bright blue eyes gives me a slam of butterflies.

"Tell me. Would you go along to another client proposal unless they spelled out exactly what *bottle* they were thinking of? Exactly what the hell they were going to make you do for them?"

I answer honestly.

"Depends on the price. And the client. Their reputation." I pause, then smile. "And how I was feeling when the proposal came through."

"What if the price was nothing more than a club visit out in

Cannes? Quite a pathetic payout compared to the big spenders, I'm sure."

I give him a wave of my hand. "The payout means absolutely nothing when it comes to you, Heath. I'd do it for free."

Josh pauses with his glass halfway to his mouth, and I feel his stare burning. My own cheeks burn up, and my heart thumps, because I've overstepped the line here. That kind of sentiment should never be spoken aloud. Clients should never be offered services for free. Not ever. That's breaking the code of conduct. And sure, we are staying in Heath Mason's villa for a token fee, not a huge one, but he is still a client and he is still 'rewarding' us on top for our services. We are still his *curvas*.

"I shouldn't have said that," I say, hating how awkward the words feel in my mouth. "Sorry, that's totally unprofessional."

Heath shrugs. "There are plenty of things that shouldn't have been said on this trip. I'm not counting. And I'm not going to hold you to it. I'm happy to keep paying for your services. The Agency will have nothing to complain about."

Urgh, I really have goofed up here. Something feels weird. Like splashing around in unfamiliar waters – a tangle of work and emotions that I don't know how the fuck to navigate.

No, the Agency won't have anything to complain about officially when it comes to Heath being a client, I know that. But this isn't about the Agency... it's about him. The niggling feeling that I don't want Heath to be paying for what should rightfully be his for free. Josh and I both want to be here, I'm just telling the truth. We'd happily be doing these 'proposals' for no fee at all, and if things were different maybe we'd even be dishing out proposals of our own right back at him.

Now *that's* something I'd like to see.

Josh's 'proposals' to Heath, giving the commands on exactly what Heath would be expected to perform for the evening, and watching Heath stew excitedly as he awaited his servitude. His desire for a *five-star* rating.

I imagine putting pen to paper for myself. I'd have so many fantasies of my own regarding my boyfriend and my onscreen idol. So many dreams to tap into…

"I mean it," Heath says, his words cutting through my thoughts and dragging me out of dream world. "The Agency will have no gripe whatsoever, Ella. There is no need to be concerned."

"I'm not concerned." I smile as I reach over and take his hand across the counter, giving his fingers a squeeze. I could elaborate so much more on how I feel about things, but it would only stir up a muddy pit of emotions that both Josh and I would get caught up in, and that's not fair. On either of us.

Or on Heath.

Josh coughs as he steps over and refills his water glass. I know from his grin that he's going to derail this avenue completely. He's good with diversions.

"Come on, Ells, be a good *curva* now and get your bladder filled. Heathy baby is going to get the night of his dreams. We're here to make sure of it."

I note how he uses the word *curva*. The accentuation spot on. I also notice the way Heath's smile disappears for just a moment. A flash of… something. *Rejection? Disappointment? Hurt?*

His smile returns in a flash, replaced by a brighter one. Just not so genuine.

"Yes, you are here to make sure of it," he says. "Want your reward tomorrow? You're going to have to earn it. It's quite a club I've got in mind for you."

Fine. Avenue sealed as it should be, so let the games begin.

We barely bother with dinner this evening, since we're all so keen to get to the action. We have some cheese, biscuits, and another load of grapes, for a laugh. I munch a load down happily, and indulge in a lovely, chilled bottle of my favourite sparkling wine from the day, but there is a parallel at play here. We are necking the water back like there's no tomorrow.

The sun is only just setting when I cross my legs against the need to go and pee, it's getting that overpowering. The guys must be feeling the same since they've been knocking it back just as much as I have – but they are much more used to this game. Josh has been an entertainer a lot longer than I have. I'm still a relative newbie.

My boyfriend clocks the way my legs are positioned on the lounger. The sparkle of the fading sun on the swimming pool doesn't help me any. *Water...*

"You need to piss, don't you?" he asks me, his tone dark and sultry. He pops another grape into his mouth, munching slowly as I squirm. "What do you want your beautiful curva to do, Heathy baby? She's running out of composure." His eyes meet mine. "Admit it, Ells. Tell Heath how much you're aching to take a piss right now. Does it ache? It aches, doesn't it?"

His words only make the strain worse.

"You must need to go, too," I say, but Josh shakes his head. "Not just yet. Practice makes perfect."

Yeah, just as I thought. These two are pros. I'm still a filthy little novice.

Josh laughs a dirty laugh.

"Lift your skirt up and spread your legs for Heath. Tell him how much you need to piss, and ask him kindly for your next instruction."

Josh is such a natural when it comes to taking the lead. He's smirking at Heath, beckoning him closer, so that our client can get an up close look at my predicament. They sit on a lounger together, staring at me as I hitch my cami dress up. I've got a pair of lace panties on underneath. Spreading my legs is so hard that I have to clench my muscles like a vice to avoid soaking the panties right through. I'm like a fucking dam set to burst.

"I've got an idea for our sweet curva," Heath says to Josh. "A lovely little party trick to get us started."

"Please get it started quick," I groan. "Or I might bust before I get to perform."

"Nah," Josh says, and takes my glass of wine from the table, still half full. "You underestimate yourself. Knock that back before you do a thing. Show how willing you are."

I don't want a single sip of drink, I want to pee so bad, but I do as I'm told anyway – already heady on a decent few glasses of the decadent wine Heath treated me to.

"Strip," Heath says as he takes my empty glass from me. "I want you naked before you spill a drop from that sweet cunt of yours."

I race to do as instructed. I tug my cami dress up and over my head and toss it aside, and unclip my bra to launch that, too. Thank fuck today's basic disguise outfit makes it easy. My panties are harder to remove, my bladder ready to blow as I wriggle out of them and cast them to the side of the lounger.

"What now?" I ask, crossing my legs again.

I'm not sure what to expect when Heath steps up to the top of the lounger and clicks the backrest up so it's practically upright. Josh seems to be on the same page, though. He gives an *ah* in approval and gets up to join our client, taking my ankles as Heath takes my wrists.

Then they manoeuvre me.

They turn me upside down, so my shoulders are where my butt was sitting, my legs hooked over the top of the lounger. And I get it. From this position, I'm going to piss all over myself when I go.

My big tits loll against my chin, and they are going to be nothing short of a chasm, directing the river… right onto my face.

And into my open mouth.

"You can sample yourself first, curva," Heath says. "Show me how good that wine tastes now it's flowing out the other end of you. But piss slowly. Gently. Savour every sip."

I'm not sure I'm going to be able to piss gently, since I need to go so fucking bad. I whimper when Heath spreads my pussy lips, and gives an *mmm* as he strokes my piss hole.

"Gently, curva," he says again, and I try.

I take a deep breath before I let myself go, and the first burst of piss shoots free, splashing down onto my stomach.

"Steady," Heath says. "Like a babbling brook, if you will. Think of your piss hole as a little fountain, flowing to your eager mouth."

Oh fuck, the filth of his words makes my clit spark. I adore being exposed and treated like such a dirty little slut. One more burst of piss and I do my all to keep the flow steady. It splashes down on my belly, and I use my tits to catch the flow, holding them together so the piss dribbles down a chute of cleavage to the destination.

I catch my own stream of piss with my open mouth as the guys watch me, smiling down from above as Heath keeps my cunt spread.

"Such a gorgeous fucking view," Heath says, and I gargle my first mouthful. It doesn't taste anything like wine, but that's fine by me. I swallow it down and smile a dirty smile up at them regardless.

"Touch me," I say before I open my mouth for the next stream, and Heath thumbs my clit before sliding two fingers into my pussy. He curves them forward, which only makes my pissing feel more intense. Incredible bastard.

Josh is surprisingly quiet for Josh. He looks between me and Heath with a smile on his face, a voyeur as Heath keeps control of me.

With Heath's fingers in my pussy the river flows wilder. Piss splashes off my tits and over my face, and I'm soaked in seconds, my piss stinging my eyes as it splashes.

"Go help her," Heath tells Josh, and my boyfriend appears to the side of me, kneeling down on the tiles to grip my face.

"Keep your mouth open," he says, and I nod as I do as I'm told.

He lifts my head forward, and supports the back, and it helps. More of the stream lands in my mouth, my tongue lolling and greedy as I splutter.

"Fuck her harder," Josh tells Heath. "Make her feel it."

Heath buries two more fingers in my pussy. It makes me ache… deep… and sets the flow loose. Truly loose…

I'm floating free as I fully express myself, spilling a cascade of piss like the fountain Heath wanted. It spurts from above to run like a waterfall down over my tits. A torrent of rapids splashing over rocks to end up in the hungry well of my open mouth.

"Good girl," Josh says, and laps at my wet cheek. "Fuck, yes, that tastes so good. You're lucky you get one whole round for yourself."

I never thought I'd feel lucky to get to drink one whole load of my own piss while it spills all over me, but I do feel lucky. It's not the taste, it's the attention. The pride in the filth I feel performing for Heath… and for my filthy boyfriend.

It's a relief for the true *curva* side of me to come back to the fore. I'm nothing but a hardcore entertainer again, and Heath is nothing but a client. I do his bidding for my reward, and I'll take whatever I'm given to serve him.

I piss until there's nothing left, Heath's four fingers still buried in my cunt to the knuckles.

"You're such a dirty mess," he tells me as I dribble and run dry. "That's why you're so high up my list, sweet curva. You're so good at what you do."

"Please, sir, come and make me dirtier," I say, and open my mouth for some more. It's his piss I want next. I want him like a fresh river, right into my open mouth. But he shakes his head.

"No, no. I have other plans for that, dirty girl. You'll have to wait."

"Damn," I say, and let the guys help spin me back around, so I'm lying back on my piss-soaked lounger, my hair a sopping mess as I relax back into position.

And then I drink more water.

More water and more wine.

The sun goes down, until we're in twilight, and my hair is still damp when we head back inside.

Both of the guys' bladders must be set to burst, seriously. I predict we'll be heading straight for the main bathroom, but Heath clicks his fingers and points down at the kitchen floor.

"Down there, curva. It's time for me to use the toilet." I drop to my knees, expecting him to use my mouth, but he shakes his head. "On all fours, please. Ass in the air."

He drops down on his knees behind me, and oh my fucking God. It's clear what *bottle* he was talking of filling up earlier when he spreads my ass cheeks as wide as they can go. I clench and wink my asshole at him.

"Don't tease. It's so fucking hard to piss with a hard-on," he says, and nudges the head of his dick inside my ass. "But I think I'll manage it just fine."

Yes, he will. He's solid and straining.

I adore the sensation of a warm enema, but when it's an enema of piss from Heath Mason's barbelled cock, it's a whole new league. I grunt and groan, begging for *more, more, more* as his hot piss fills my ass.

"Don't spill any," Heath says. "Don't you dare spill any on the kitchen floor, curva. Or I'll make you lick it clean."

I'm tempted to spill some, just so I get the punishment.

"Your turn, Josh," Heath says when he's done, and Josh takes his place. A fresh hard cock working its way into my sloshing ass. I'm not sure how much more I can handle inside me, but I'll take it with everything I've got.

"So much to give you," Josh says as he fills me up with round two. "Good job the *bottle* can go nice and deep, Ella. So fucking deep and dirty."

This should be so fucking gross, yet it's anything but. It gives me tingles upon tingles.

I'm going to have both guys' piss in my ass, filled to the brim, and it feels so good I can't resist using my fingers to play with myself.

I'm a human toilet. My ass is a toilet. It's so fucking sick, it's beautiful.

"What a good girl, you took it all," Josh says as he pulls out.

"What next?" I ask Heath, twisting my head to the side to stare up at him.

"What's next is that you crawl over to the table like a dirty curva, and you keep your pretty ass in the air for when we need to use the *bottle* again."

"But I can't..." I tell him. "I can't take any more."

Josh laughs. "Oh, baby, you can. Hardcorers take plenty. It's time to get practising."

He knows full well they are the words I need to spur me on.

I crawl over to the table on a mission as Heath grabs more wine. I stay on the floor with my ass in the air while they laugh and drink, saying *thank you* every time Heath graces me with a glug of wine straight from the bottle.

I'm nervous when it's time for them to fill me up with round two. I'm so full that it's already hurting – gravity working its magic to let their piss run deep inside. Josh goes first this time. He leans forward to watch me grimace as he fills me.

"Don't clench, Ella, just take it. Loosen up, let it all the way in."

"I can't..."

"Trust me, baby, you can. And remember, I know how it feels. Oh fuck, how I know how it feels."

I wonder how many times Josh has been in my position. A human toilet with his ass in the air.

I want to be a good slut for him as well as for Heath. I want my inner slut to reign proud, and show myself in my full glory – a hardcorer to the extreme. Born to top the leaderboard.

So I do loosen up. I do what Josh tells me, and embrace the filthy sensation for the bliss that it is. I take the guys' piss as deep as it'll go, and I thank them for using me. I thank them for the sensation of feeling so fucking full. So fucking used. So fucking filthy.

And then, when they give me permission, I crawl with my full sloshing ass clenched tight, all the way to the bathroom. I squat in the shower over the plughole with a smile on my face, like they tell me to – with both men watching as the *bottle* gets emptied.

Holy fuck, how it streams out of me.

They crouch down low so they can see, and the glee in Heath's dirty eyes is unparalleled.

Piss play is definitely his thing.

"Do it," he says. "Let it all out. Push as hard as you can."

I blank my mind to everything but the sensation as I let loose. Four loads of piss from the depths of my fucking ass, still warm and nurtured from the past few hours.

I've never felt anything so revoltingly hot in my life.

Freedom through exposure. Freedom without restraint. Freedom that gives me a smile on my face at the sheer thought of what the guys must be witnessing as my inner *bottle* flows free.

"Filthy little curva," Heath says, and crawls forward to kiss me.

I'm lost to the sensations of being a filthy *curva*. I'm heady and desperate, too wound up for it to end.

"I want more," I tell him. "Please tell me you have more for me. Please."

"Oh, we have more, curva. Just like you do."

He gets up and switches on the hot shower, and I stand to join both men. A tangle of limbs and lips as the remnants of their piss washes down the drain. Such a waste…

At least there's plenty more to come.

Mouthful after mouthful of *wine* from every angle, and this time we all savour it – like we did with the beautiful varieties at the vineyard.

I think my favourite tonight is Josh's actually, but it's a close call...

Luckily, we have an abundance of wine to give us so much more *wine*. More and more spilling free as the night goes on, all of us glugging back water along with the alcohol.

So much for Heath's *no spillage* on the kitchen floor rule earlier.

It's my turn to be the voyeur as the guys get caught up together for one particularly explosive spray. They laugh as they stand and hose each other, both of them straining for the highest reach. I'm laughing along with them until it gets serious, and Josh grabs Heath's piss-wet hair to throw him to the ground. Poor Heath lands hard on the sopping wet floor tiles.

"I'm not wasting any more. Open your filthy fucking mouth and be a *curva* yourself, baby. Drink my piss and thank me for it," Josh says.

Oh, fuck, his tone is so fucking strong.

I rub my sopping pussy as Heath scrambles to his knees.

"It's my proposal, remember?"

Josh smirks a filthy smirk. "Yeah, but we all know this is how you like it. Dish it out all you like, Heath, but you'll always be a dirty slut yourself, begging for just as much."

Josh has him nailed. A moan from Heath, and he opens his mouth wide, catching Josh's spray like it's the fountain of life. My boyfriend fucks his face as he's pissing – a sloshing stream spurting from Heath's lips with every thrust.

I put one of my feet up on the dining table, legs spread as I play and watch. It's so hot, it gives me butterflies upon butterflies.

I'm almost at the brink when Josh runs out of piss and orders Heath up to his feet.

"My turn," Josh says. "Give it to me."

Josh works his mouth up and down Heath's straining cock as Heath curses, finding it hard to piss. He takes hold of Josh's head, and braces himself, trying to go… and it works. I flinch at the first burst, so fierce it makes Josh retch.

But not for long.

Josh is a pro, after all.

I watch the guys playing. Pissing and kissing and tumbling onto the floor together in the aftermath.

I feel like a kinky ghost on the sidelines, watching with a smile on my face and my fingers on my clit until Heath clicks *his* fingers and summons me over.

The floor is like a fucking lake when I get down on my knees and crawl over to them.

"I want to come in the fucking toilet bowl," Heath tells me, and the sparkle in his filthy eyes is full of sin. "Another round of fill the bottle, only this time, it'll be with *cream* and not *wine*."

Both guys take it in turns with my empty asshole – so sensitive after so much use earlier.

"Please…" I groan. "Be brave boys and fuck me both at once. You managed my cunt. Now manage my ass."

I know they are looking at each other contemplating it.

"Please!" I say again. "Go in sync, stretch me to bursting. I don't care. It's ok."

They answer without words – Josh taking up position on the floor and hoisting me onto him. I loll back and relax, with my head against his shoulder and my back to his clammy chest. There's a smile on my face as I feel them align themselves – their piss covered dicks thick and fucking hard.

Hard and ready to blow.

Shit, how it fucking hurts when they push in as one. It sears like a bitch, straining so hard I must be tearing. Josh restrains me, hooking his arms under mine as I wriggle.

"Stay fucking still," he hisses into my ear, and I nod for him.

I stay still like a good curva and take the savage intrusion... just like I wanted it.

I'm a greedy bitch tonight, and I want the first of everything. I want to be the receiver of the cream before the guys get to play. Oh, how I'm desperate to see their hunger.

It'll be a much thicker river when I push this juicy treat out for them.

I come just thinking about it, sandwiched between the men of my dreams, while my asshole takes their dessert. We'll all be licking our lips for a taste of it.

Thank fuck there'll be enough to share.

We'll definitely be having seconds.

fourteen

The reward can't be right. No way. I mean, it's amazing, but he must have got it wrong.

Heath has picked out a mighty fine restaurant in Cannes and a mega cool looking club to hang out in later. He shows us the pictures eagerly. But there will be one thing missing.

Him.

Heath isn't planning on coming with us this evening.

What the holy fuck?

"I could easily get recognised," he says when I raise my eyebrows. "Believe me, Ella, I don't want that. I don't want a hoard of paparazzi at the gates, and people out to take a snap of me wherever I turn. It's one thing in London, but out here…"

"You could go in disguise," I say. "Nobody would have recognised you yesterday, not a chance. You barely even looked like you."

He smiles. "That was at a vineyard in the middle of nowhere with about ten members of staff present. Not in town on a Friday night while the masses are out to play."

I look at Josh. He has pitted brows, staring at Heath as though it's a travesty.

"Ells and I can head out to a fancy restaurant and a club whenever we want to, Heath. And I don't want to sound ungrateful, not at all, but we're here for *you*. We want to be with *you*."

I nod along, because Josh is spot on, and I couldn't emphasise that enough. I'd adore a night out in swanky Cannes, don't get me wrong – strolling hand in hand with my boyfriend. Eating fine cuisine, and dancing the night away. But we get the opportunity for that kind of thing plenty in London. We could fly out wherever we wanted for a luxury retreat, just the two of us. Just not with Heath.

The idea of being away from our amazing client for the evening tears at my heart strings. It actually hurts.

"We've only got two nights left," I say. "Then we'll be back on a flight without you. Please, just think about coming with us. Downgrade the meal to somewhere more obscure, pick a nightclub that isn't so prestigious. Whatever, Heath, just come with us!"

Heath looks torn. "I wanted to give you the chance to experience the incredible vibe of Cannes at night. You deserve it."

"And we thank you for that, so much." I reach over the breakfast bar to grip his hand. "But honestly, we'd rather spend it with you."

He smiles. "Thank you, that's a lovely sentiment."

"It's true," Josh says. "Come on, Heathy baby, take a risk for once, will you? Are we not worth it? Stick on a cap, and we'll play it down. You'll just be a guy out with a regular couple. No big deal."

My stunning idol laughs at that.

"Josh *baby*, have you seen your girlfriend lately? You may be able to play down your incredible physique, and tone down your hair a little, but Ella? She's never going to be able to shield her beauty from the public. The tour guide was eyeing her up all the way through the vineyard yesterday."

I blush at his words. The way he looks at me with such adoration gives me a fresh lurch.

He raises my hand to his lips and kisses it.

"You two go. Have a wonderful evening."

He grabs his orange juice and wanders out towards the terrace in his swim shorts, but I hold Josh back before he has chance to accompany him.

"We're not going," I say, with a shake of my head. "No way, Josh. I'm not going out and leaving Heath here, not while the clock is ticking so fast."

His eyes lock on mine, and he ruffles my hair.

"Don't worry, baby. I'm not intending to. We have plenty of hours left before the booking, just let me lead, ok?"

I don't know what plan Josh has up his sleeve, but I'm prepared to trust him on it. He knows Heath far better than I do.

We all relax together with pastries and banter, like usual, and I take a dip in the pool as the guys sunbathe. Wow. This place truly is fucking amazing.

I fold my arms on the side of the infinity pool, and look out onto the sea, and the gorgeous sandy beach down below. Bright blues, and creamy whites. Such beauty with the full beam of the sun overhead.

I'd love to feel the sand between my toes, but more than that, I'd love to have Heath's feet walking along beside me. His toes in the sand along with mine.

If only we could break him out of his reservations, just for a while. I suspect there's more to Heath's fears than I know about, and Josh will never share that information with me. It will come from Heath, and Heath alone, when the time is right. If it ever is.

I get a horrible, horrible pang at a fresh realisation that nothing whatsoever is concrete with Heath Mason. He's a client. No matter how much I crave him, and want him, and adore him, he's just a client.

I try to push that thought aside as best I can.

We haven't been down through the gate to the beach yet, at the bottom of the villa grounds. It's been on my mind for a few days now, but the desire has been surpassed by a whole host of other *activities.* Maybe now could be the time?

I swim back to the other side of the pool to suggest a saunter, surprised to see both guys sitting upright on their loungers, their hands expressive as they engage in some kind of serious conversation. I almost turn around and swim away again, but they see me coming.

"Come on out for a second, Ella," Josh says, and I do as I'm told, scooting up the pool steps and grabbing my towel from the floor on the way.

"What is it?" I ask, and sit down beside him.

"Josh is on my case," Heath says. "He's trying to tempt me with the wonders of hitting the town with you tonight. Appealing to my more... *rational* side, as he calls it."

"One night isn't going to hurt," Josh tells him. "Seriously, will you just trust me? You're simply a guy from the TV, heading out with a couple of friends. A *couple* of friends. We won't even touch you. We'll be all over each other."

I don't know what to say, so I don't say anything at all.

"How long is it since you've been out in town?" Josh asks. "You used to enjoy it. I remember your tales."

"They were a long time ago."

"Yes, exactly! So let's make some new ones. Just for a night or so."

"Two," I butt in. "We have two nights."

Heath rolls his eyes. "Two now? So you're not just trying to wrestle me out of the villa for one night in the public eye, it's now doubled."

"Fine," Josh holds his hands up. "We'll be thinking of you."

I go to speak again, but Josh flashes me a glance. I know that glance. It means *stay quiet*.

I move to my own lounger and towel myself off, soaking in the tension between the two guys. It's burning hotter than the sun – like magma under the surface – even though Josh reaches over to pat Heath's thigh with a grin on his face.

As for Heath. He can't stop looking at Josh. He tries to relax, but his eyes keep flitting. Staring.

"What?" Josh asks, after a while.

"Nothing. I was just admiring my beautiful curves in the sun."

"Sure." Josh smirks. "Keep admiring us, then. Let us know if you want some dick or pussy from your beautiful curves, and we'll be more than happy to serve."

Josh sounds so cocky. So alive. Mesmerising in that addictive way my boyfriend behaves.

It's no surprise that Heath can't keep his eyes off him. I'm with him on that score.

We have another few glasses of orange juice and a fruit salad, and the topic of our upcoming reward isn't raised again for hours. Not until Heath gives a sigh as Josh takes a dip in the pool.

"Damn him," Heath says to me, then shoots me a grin. "And damn you, too."

"What for?"

He leans back, his arms folded behind his head.

"I want to come with you tonight. I really fucking do."

"Well, I'd hope so, since we're going somewhere so amazing."

"It's not about *somewhere* so amazing. It's coming with you." Heath pauses. "I want to do it."

I shuffle on my lounger.

"For real? Oh my God. Are you going to do it? Are you going to come?"

He sighs. "I shouldn't."

I use my opportunity as Josh swims a length.

"I know things must be crazy for you, Heath, being a huge celebrity and all that, but I'm sure Josh is right. We can keep it low key."

He looks right at me. "I hope so, because there's no way I'll be able to watch you walk out of the door without me. It would be too fucking hard."

"What's that?" Josh asks, arriving back at our side of the pool.

I can hardly contain my excitement.

"Heath says he's coming with us tonight! He's coming out in Cannes with us!"

Josh is straight over to the steps, not bothering to towel himself off before he races over and launches himself on top of Heath on the lounger. He peppers his cheek with wet kisses, and Heath laughs with an *easy, tiger!* But Josh doesn't go easy. His cheek kisses turn to lip kisses, his smile beaming as he brushes our client's hair away from his face and looks him straight in the eyes.

"I knew you could do it. I'm so proud of you, *Heathy baby*."

"Fuck off," Heath groans. "It's not a scout's award, Josh. I just said I'm heading out for a meal."

"And a club. You are coming to the club, aren't you? If you think we're gonna wave you off in a cab while we hit the party scene, you're going to have to wrestle us away from you before you go."

"We'll see," Heath says, then lands a kiss on my boyfriend's mouth. "No promises."

"Sure. No promises. Cool, ok, whatever."

Josh grinds against Heath, cocks clearly straining through their swimming shorts, and Heath moans, urging Josh on a little until he pushes him off with a *fuck*.

"What?" Josh asks, as Heath gets up from the lounger.

Yeah, his dick is hard. Really fucking hard.

"Hold off," Heath says. "I have things to do first."

"Things that trump getting your cock out?" Josh laughs. "They must be high priority."

I want to play with the pair of them myself, right fucking now, but Heath holds up a hand.

"Since I'm now coming along, I have some *amendments* to make. Urgent ones."

"To the booking? That's cool," Josh says. "We'll go wherever you want. No problem."

Heath shakes his head, a smile lighting up his gorgeous face.

"No, my darling curvas. The locations can stay as they are, I'll just add a plus one online. I'm about to amend the proposal."

The proposal.

My heart races.

"Don't even ask," Heath says and raises a finger before I start to quiz him. "You only have yourselves to blame for this. Don't say I didn't warn you."

I sure hope his warning is as ominous as it sounds.

I'll be ready for it.

The atmosphere is buzzing beyond belief as we get ready together. So much for Heath binding his hair up under a cap and hiding behind sunglasses. He's gone all out for the occasion. His hair is sleek and smooth, hanging perfectly down his back, and he's suited and booted like a dream. Black suit, white shirt, and a dark burgundy bow tie symbolic of the Count. Josh is wearing a black suit and purple tie, looking gorgeous with the purple streak in his hair on display, and as for me?

I've gone all out to impress both my client and my adoring boyfriend.

I've chosen my red satin number, figure hugging, with drapes to the floor and a lovely long split to my thigh. I have stilettos that complement it perfectly, and black elbow length gloves that accentuate my gothic makeup just so. Yeah, this will cut it in Cannes. At least, I hope so.

We are one hell of a trio when we get into the back of the cab together. I'm between the two guys and feel Heath take a deep breath when we leave his drive. He really is out of his comfort zone, no doubt about that.

And he's doing it for us.

What a gesture.

But his demeanour changes somehow when the sprawling modern villas disappear behind us and the heat and life of Cannes swallow us up in the cab. Heath loosens up and comes alive beside me, scoping out the view from the cab window like he's a kid at a fairground.

"You alright?" I ask him.

"Yeah, I'm fine. I forgot how incredible the place is."

"Good job you're about to get a reminder then, isn't it?"

He's smiling when he looks at me.

"Yes. Maybe it is."

Heath doesn't look half as awkward or terrified as I expected him to when we pull up outside the restaurant – Café Belle Époque. It's almost as though his public persona has taken control as he steps out of the cab and helps me up. But there's more to his persona than the regalness of the perfect smile on his face, and his Count-like demeanour. He's still got the regular, down to earth *Heathy baby* sparkle in his icy-blue eyes as he looks at me and Josh. The undertone of *him* sounds loud and clear to me as he presents the door to the restaurant.

"Let's get dining," he says.

I take Josh's hand as the server shows us to our table, in the back corner of the eatery – making it clear that we are a couple out with a celebrity friend of ours, and nothing more. No dodgy business. No threesomes. No *curvas* out with their client.

People look at Heath as we walk along, sure, talking in hushed whispers as they gawp, but nobody jumps out with a squeal and a *Count, I love you!* Not like they would at a Nighttime Whispers convention or a night out in Camden.

We are sitting happily in a corner booth, sipping on champagne and perusing the menu when a figure steps up to us and clears his throat. I smile politely, having no idea who the hell the old guy is, but Heath clearly does. He leaps up from his seat and pulls the man into a hug with a Clément!

"I didn't expect to see you still working here!" Heath says as he pulls away, but the man nods.

"Oui, oui. I have never left. I have been waiting for you. I thought that maybe my escargots de Bourgogne had scared you away."

"No, never. They are delicious!"

The warmth in Heath's eyes as he sits back down knocks the wind from my lungs. It's weird, to see him so alive and buzzing outside of the villa walls. I squeeze Josh's hand under the table, and his fingers grip mine in response – the silent gesture conveying unspoken words.

I'm so glad Heath came.

And I'm also so glad that *Clément* put in an appearance. The pair of them talked like true old friends.

Heath's eyes look almost watery as he grins across at us, and then he laughs.

"Thank you," he says. "For making me come. Tonight, not just in general."

"We're the ones who owe you, not the other way around. Cheers to us," Josh says and raises his glass.

It's a *cheers* from me, too. I'd give all the *cheers* in creation for moments like this. Amazing doesn't even come close to cutting it.

Heath leans across the table towards us, his eyes full of delight.

"You must try the escargots de Bourgogne. They are out of this fucking world."

"Can't wait," Josh says.

"Me, neither," I add.

"Seriously, guys. Those snails are truly –" He does a chef's kiss. "Magnifique! You are in for a treat."

A waiter appears from nowhere.

"Your cocktails, monsieur."

From the tray he's holding in one palm, he places three huge bowl glasses on the table, filled with yellow liquid, and pineapple chunks, and what looks like gold flakes swirling about. They're topped with crushed ice and a cherry.

"Merci," Heath says and the waiter bows and walks away.

"Ordered in advance," Heath says and picks up a glass, eyeing its contents. "It's Krug champagne, limoncello, pineapple pieces, and they're real gold flakes. It's called *Liquid Gold*. Rather fitting, I thought. And rather special, since they're five hundred euros a pop. Bottoms up!"

He takes a sip, so does Josh. And so do I.

And I get a tingle all the way up my spine as I savour the suited Heath Mason truly coming into himself. *Magnifique* kinda sums him up.

"Wow," Josh says, "that's really good shit."

Heath chuckles. "I have to agree. Maybe we'll just stick to these all night."

"Honestly, Heath," Josh says, "this is a real treat. Cheers!"

"Cheers!" Heath says, clinking glasses. "This is just the start, my friends." He turns to me with a grin. "Bottoms up, Ells. There's lots more treats to come."

"Cheers, *my friend*." I lift my glass and take a sip.

Holy hell, there is so much I can't wait for tonight.

The meal.

The magnifique snails.

The club.

The *magnifique* company.

And last but not least – the *amended* proposal…

fifteen

FRIDAY

I want to see my special curva in slutty action, to get a taste for just how sterling a performer she is when she is in the hands of other clients.
Only these will not be 'clients' tonight, they will be men, chosen by me.
Two of them at once, to be precise. You will be performing with two random 'clients' selected by me this evening,
Ella. You will be given a brief to follow – as you would with any other proposal. These men are in for a lucky gift this evening.
Any man would find such a beautiful curva hard to resist, so there will be plenty of options to choose from. I will select the clients, and the proposal will be underway as soon as I give the word – with instructions given as to what services you will be providing.
Make it authentic, sweet curva. I will be watching. And so will your adoring boyfriend.
I'm curious to observe how much he enjoys the experience alongside me.
Please deliver us a five-star performance, and nothing less.
I'm sure you will.

Proposal duration – three hours
Reward – a trip out on the wonderful French Riveria tomorrow. I have booked an afternoon yacht voyage.
For all three of us.

. . .

I don't know which part of Heath's proposal I'm more shocked by as I read it through at the restaurant. The fact that I'll be 'performing' with strangers in front of both my client and my boyfriend, or the reward itself.

Heath will be coming with us on the yacht tomorrow. A yacht, with Heath Mason on it.

He handed me the envelope once we were finished up with dessert, passing it under the table.

I examine the paper the proposal is written on, being sure to keep it hidden from prying eyes. He's added that last part, about the three of us. I can see the change in the pen colour.

I give him a smirk across the table, suspecting he scribbled that extra little line during his bathroom break earlier.

"What do you think, sweet curva?" he asks me.

"I'm more than happy to oblige. And as for the reward. Wow. I guess being out and about has definitely had an impact on you."

Heath leans back in his seat. The cocktails have been flowing nicely, and the wonderful upmarket thrum of the restaurant has been putting him at ease, little by little. It's been so nice to witness.

"Yes, it's certainly had an impact." He smiles. "I like it."

"Good," I reply. "Because I like it, too." I take Josh's arm to the side of me. "We both do."

Heath locks eyes with Josh.

"And how do you think you will enjoy the rest of it, Josh? How do you feel about Ella performing later this evening?"

Josh pats his lips with a napkin. "Piece of cake. No problem whatsoever. Ells will nail it."

"I'm not talking about Ella," Heath says. "I'm talking about you."

"Me?" Josh smirks, and flashes me a smile. "Piece of cake on that score, too. It's just work, I'm used to it."

It's when his eyes linger a little too long on mine that I register what is about to go down here. Yeah, it's work. I fuck other clients, Josh fucks other clients, and we do double bookings where we fuck clients together. But I've never been on the sidelines, watching him fuck other people without me involved. Other *women*. I haven't seen him only as a performer, pleasuring other people while I stare on mute and out of the picture.

Neither has he. The situation is the same in reverse.

The regularity of proposals has become pretty standard in our world. We wave goodbye with a *see you later, babe, earn those five stars!* We stay up, waiting for the *D&S* – Done and Safe – message to come through, all set to greet each other with kisses and hugs and congratulations. And we have after sex. Lots of after sex. But as for seeing it? In the flesh?

I dunno. It seems a bit… weird.

"It'll be cool," Josh says to me, clearly noticing my realisation. "Can't wait to see you at the top of your game. It'll be an experience."

"You've seen me at the top of my game plenty of times."

"Only when I'm part of the game."

Heath leans across the table.

"You don't have to proceed." His smile has a slight edge of nerves to it. "You can keep the reward regardless. We'll all still take the trip on the yacht tomorrow." He reaches across the table for the proposal. "Let's just forget it, shall we?"

I keep hold of the paper, looking at him as he looks at me. Trying to read him.

What is this really about? I didn't have Heath down as much of a voyeur – not outside of watching me and Josh play in front of him, so this is pretty left field.

Maybe the buzz of being in public has done something to him. Either way, he deserves his proposal, and I'm sure Josh feels the same, so I fold the proposal letter up and slip it back in the envelope. It goes in my clutch, not in his waiting hand.

"I'm doing it," I tell him.

His shoulders drop. "You really don't have to."

"I know that. But I'm doing it anyway. Just give me the instructions when it's time."

Heath's gaze switches to Josh. "How about you? How do you feel?"

Josh is so chill as he takes a sip of his cocktail.

"Like I said, it'll be cool. An experience."

"I hope so," Heath says, and calls over the server for the bill.

I've been feeling anonymous in Cannes, largely in the cocoon of Heath's amazing villa, but I feel the attention a lot more as we leave the restaurant, as though the bubble has been burst. I noticed Heath getting stares, whispers and wide eyes on the way in, sure, but I'm far more aware of them now. I feel on display myself along with him as I walk at his side, and I'm not sure I like the sensation. Maybe it's the proposal lying ahead… or maybe it's just how it is.

For me, it's just one night. For him, he's in the spotlight, everywhere he goes.

It's not just Heath Mason people are looking at as we walk from Café Belle Époque to a swanky club around the corner. They are looking at me and Josh, too. Examining us. I grip my boyfriend's hand and put a big grin on my face, trying to live up to the status of the celebrity masterpiece at our side, and I get it. I do.

I finally feel what it must be like for him, everywhere he goes.

Women stare at me in particular, looking me up and down before whispering and giggling. Judging. Gossiping. I dunno. It brings back just a touch of my self-consciousness from when I was a nobody, living in London squalor while Connor took the spotlight on stage. I never felt good enough. Worthy enough. Deserving enough.

But things are very, very different now.

I'm a very, very different woman to the sad girl I used to be. I *am* good enough. I *am* worthy enough. And I always will be – walking at the side of Heath Mason or not.

It's an honour to be at the side of a man so incredible as him AND at the side of a man so incredible as Josh. My smile notches up, naturally, because I am not the old Ella anymore. I glow with pride from deep within.

Fuck anyone who wants to shoot any of us down. They can fuck right off.

"Are you alright?" Heath asks, pulling me to the side when we reach the entrance to Le Mirage – one of the swankiest clubs in the whole of Cannes.

I laugh, resisting the urge to stroke his cheek. "I should be asking you that question, not the other way around."

Josh still has my hand, and squeezes tight.

"We're all alright, Heath. Stop worrying and start enjoying things. You got this. We all have."

The sparkle in Heath's eyes lights up my whole world.

"I've been enjoying this more than you could ever imagine. It's one of the greatest decisions I've ever made."

Josh chuckles. "See if you're still saying that at the end of the night." Heath's eyes widen until Josh pats him on the back. "Joke. It's gonna be cool. It's all gonna be real fucking great, just feel that vibe. It's rocking."

I *can* feel the vibe. The thump of the bass booming loud. The cocktails have gone to my head, and my feet are itching to dance in my stilettos. My whole body is screaming for more, more, more. I don't ever want the night to end.

The filthy proposal will only be a part of it.

One I'm going to be proud of.

We don't slip into the club unnoticed. One of the bouncers clocks Heath in an instant, and the rail is opened for us, letting us straight inside. We're led upstairs to the VIP balcony, and a server comes over to us especially, seeking us out in the crowd.

Heath orders more swanky cocktails. Passionfruit and strawberry something this time. Really fucking nice, whatever they are. I wouldn't want to see the price tag on these. He must have spent thousands in the restaurant already.

We dance together in a little trio, with our glasses in the air, revelling in the energy around us. The dim lighting makes it easier for the anonymity to swallow us back up into its safety net – the spotlights all focused downstairs.

I make sure that my hands are all over Josh, not Heath. We don't want any rumours flying around he'll have to contend with.

I'm just a girl out with her boyfriend, both of us friends with Heath Mason and nothing more.

Such a shame it can't be more. I'd be the happiest girl in the world to be able to express my true feelings for Heath as well as Josh. To be free. *In love.*

Ouch. The thought is too much.

I dismiss it – putting it down to cocktails and ambience and shoving it back in my internal shadows where it belongs.

"How about the proposal?" I ask Heath when we're done dancing to another track. "Better get things moving. Any more cocktails and I'll hardly be able to walk on these bad boys." I lift up a heel.

"I'm sure you'll manage, princess," he says – then seems to forget himself as he takes my hand and leads both me and Josh over to the edge of the balcony. His need for anonymity has taken a back seat. Again, probably down to cocktails and ambience. Such killers.

Whoa, the place has been filling up. There are people everywhere down there – suits and designer dresses galore.

Heath seems to be scouting the dancefloor. I watch his eyes as they skirt and ponder. So addictive.

He leans into me, so I can just about hear his words over the music.

"In the corner, over there at the far side of the bar. A group of guys, clearly on the lookout. The ladies' bathroom is behind them, so it'll be easy for you to make an *introduction*. Go, sweet curva. Pick two of your choice and take them for a walk, along the glorious sand towards the villa. Such privacy there."

I get it. I'll end up by the villa… and most likely by the secret entrance to the beach. Very private.

And very clever.

"We'll be watching," Heath adds. "Give us the performance of a lifetime, please. Be a dirty curva, and act like it." He reaches a hand into his pocket and puts something in mine.

I glance down to find rubbers in my grip. Four. Ok, wow, he does want a performance. I slip them into my clutch.

"Two guys, yeah?"

"Yes, two."

"Any preferences? Want me to do anything in particular?"

"I'll leave that up to you. Enjoy."

"Ok. I'll see you later."

I turn to my boyfriend, whispering an *I'm off, love you*, and giving him a kiss before I retreat from the pair of them. It feels bizarre to be leaving them behind, knowing they'll have their eyes on me from the balcony. And who knows where else?

I imagine they'll be following.

Fuck, I'm going to give them a show.

Heath totally deserves it.

I weave my way to the ladies', taking my time so that I know Heath and Josh will have located me. I imagine them watching from up above, and it feels… good. Yeah. It feels good.

I prep myself in the bathroom, topping up my deep scarlet lipstick and planning the route ahead.

I know the way… once we're out on the front, the beach will lead us all the way along the boulevard, and out towards Heath's place.

A group of women join me in the bathroom, set for some freshening up themselves. They stare at me like I'm some kind of zoo exhibit and my cheeks burn in horror, because fuck, they must have seen me with Heath! They're speaking French, so I don't understand what they're saying, but when one of them gets out their phone and starts angling it in my direction, I know it's time to bolt. Right now. I have to get my mission underway and get the hell out of here.

My adrenaline is pumping harder than the bass when I rush out of the bathroom and barge into the crowd of guys Heath was pointing at. I act like I've slipped, grabbing hold of a bulky member of their gang, giggling as he holds me steady.

He's a great barrier for the women leaving the bathroom. They walk on by without a sight of me. Thank fuck for that.

"You ok?" the bulky blond asks, and it's a relief to hear his cockney accent. Flirting with him in my native tongue will be so much easier.

I make a bold move, opting for casual – a casual girl in glamorous clothing.

"Yeah, I'm cool. Just drunk and fucking horny." I laugh. "Much harder to pull anyone in this kind of place than it is back home. I won this flashy French holiday a few months ago and got dressed up for the part and everything. Thought I'd be getting laid by now."

His eyes light up as he looks me up and down.

"I don't think you'll have any trouble getting laid, sweetheart."

I laugh again. "Is that an offer? If it is, I'll take it."

He laughs along with me, shaking his head in obvious disbelief. "Don't you even want a drink first?"

I lean into him. "Nah. My friend has already fucked off with a guy and ditched me. Can't be assed with another cocktail. They cost a bloody fortune."

He looks flustered, like a duck out of water, and one of his friends raises an eyebrow, obviously wondering what the fuck is

THE NAUGHTY WEEK

happening. The thumping bass is a blessing. It drowns out our conversation.

"You really want to leave? Now? For sex?"

"Sure do." I run my hand down his posh shirted chest, and it feels weird knowing my boyfriend is watching from up above. "There is, um, one condition though." I side eye the friend of his who raised an eyebrow. He's hot. Tanned and dark haired. Confident. He reeks of swagger.

They'll be a good pair. A good *enough* pair. "I want two at once." I bite on my lip as I lean into my conquest. "Seriously, I'm such a horny bitch. I can't get enough." I put my hand to my mouth as though I've revealed the secret of a lifetime. "Sorry. Cocktails talking. Cocktails and the truth."

Buff blond raises his eyebrows, and I worry I've pushed it too far.

"You want to fuck me *and* Marcus? Now?"

All or nothing...

"Shit," I hold up my hands. "That sounds bad, doesn't it? Sorry, I'm just a dirty bitch. Ignore me, I'll move on."

I make to step away, but he grabs me by the arm. Tightly.

Yes. I've got him.

"Hang on there. What's your name?"

I almost say *Holly*. But no, that doesn't feel right. "Lucy."

"Lucy?"

"Yep. And I'm out to be a *lucky* Lucy tonight."

"I, um..." Poor buff blond stutters as he tries to weigh up the situation. "Ok, I'll ask him. Just wait right here."

He gestures for *Marcus* to join him a few steps away, and I chance a glance up at the balcony. I feel so fucking vulnerable down here. Vulnerable at the prospect of failure more than anything, because if I have played it too fucking quick with Blond and Marcus, then I'll look like such a tit in front of Heath and Josh.

I suck in some breaths, because if I do get the chance with

Blond and Marcus, I'm going to get my act together and up my game. Earning five stars has been so easy this week that I've become comfortable. *Too* comfortable.

I'm an entertainer in this bar tonight, just like the entertainer I am back at home.

Thank the heavens that both Buff Blond and Marcus appear before me with dirty grins on their faces.

"Hey, Lucy," Marcus says, another cockney.

I shoot him a drunk, flirty smile.

"Hi there, Marcus. You going to come with us? I'm sure you've been told what a horny cow I am. Sorry, this isn't my general, uh, territory. I'm from the East End."

"No problem with that," he says. "We were looking for a companion tonight anyway. I'm happy to come along, if Ben is alright with sharing."

Marcus and Ben.

"You've made my night," I laugh. "Just a few things, though."

I pull both guys closer to me, my heart thumping as I think of my onlookers upstairs.

"I like it dirty. Like real fucking dirty. I'm talking on the beach. I love getting fucked on the beach. I love cock down my throat. And I love it in my fucking ass as well. Think you can handle that?"

I flutter my lashes as I pull away, using my looks to my advantage as I hold my shoulders back – the huge rack of my cleavage on proud display.

Marcus swallows, and Ben runs his fingers through his blond hair, and I'm good enough at this game by now to know both of them have raging hard-ons.

Yeah, I've succeeded.

I *will* succeed.

"I'm sure we can handle that," Ben says, and he wastes no fucking time getting on with it. Maybe he thinks I'm a fucking headcase, high or trashed on cocktails, and it's clear he sure doesn't want to miss the opportunity.

They push past their friends with slaps on the shoulders and me in tow. I wave goodbyes to the randoms around me, and strut along, following their lead.

As much as the balcony calls me, I don't look up. I don't dare. I don't want to risk so much as a glance in Heath Mason's direction now I'm a slut on duty.

The guys slow down when we're around the back of the club and heading towards the beachfront. Ben lets go of my hand when he realises I'm not a bitch on a high who is going to make a run for it now we're out the door.

"East End?" he asks, and I nod.

"Yeah, couldn't believe it when I won the online raffle thing I entered. I only sent a text as a joke."

"Ah. You entered one of those?"

I nod as though I'm proud. "Best thing I've ever done. Only did it because I was drunk." I pause and give them a twirl. "Look at the outfit I got out of it, too."

Both men laugh. Their suits are designer. They certainly didn't win their trip to Cannes in a raffle.

"You look incredible in that outfit," Marcus says. "I cannot wait to see you out of it."

I point up at the moon. "Good job it's a full one. You'll get to see plenty on the beach."

We keep walking.

"We don't need to fuck on the beach, Lucy. I have a hotel suite nearby," Ben says.

I shake my head with a laugh. "No way! It's one of my bucket list things. Sex on a beach with two at once."

I'm glad it's late enough that these guys have had enough drink to loosen them up. I can't imagine them considering this absurdity in the cold light of day, but they are well up for it right now. They take one of my hands each as we stroll together with the beach to our right, the waves gently lapping.

I wonder if Heath and Josh are following us, or if they are on their way back to the villa.

I'll make sure I'm in full view, regardless.

I wish I had taken advantage of the opportunity for another drink or two from Ben as we walk along. The night air is beautifully warm, but it's sobering, and my senses get heightened with every step.

These aren't clients as such. They are clients *because* of a client. And it's different.

They are strangers without safety checks, or a proposal laid out to stick to. Just two guys with a girl they think wants filthy sex with them as a bucket list item on a glorious beach in Cannes.

I do have a safety check in place though, and my gut instinct is sure on that. I have two safety checks in place, in fact. Josh and Heath, and no doubt wherever the proposal goes tonight, they will make sure I come out of it ok.

It takes me by surprise when Ben takes a step away from me and looks me up and down.

"You said you're Lucy, right?"

"Yeah. Lucy Louise."

"That's quite a name."

I laugh. "Yeah, my mum thought Lucy-Lou sounded cute. I don't think she'd see me as cute right now, though."

"You look familiar," he says. "Sure you weren't on one of those reality TV shows as well as winning a prize?"

I get a zip of horror as he examines me, because FUCK, maybe he saw me with Heath earlier.

Damn, this is hard.

"I wish!" I exclaim. "Man, I'd love that. Put me on Love Island any day of the week. I'd be in the hideaway every single night I was in there."

He laughs along, and I relax. I have to focus.

He didn't see me with Heath. Neither of them did. I'm just being paranoid.

"This part of the beach suit you?" Marcus asks, once the brightly lit streets of Cannes disappear behind us. We are on the deluxe villa street now, but we're not there yet… not close enough to our destination.

"Not yet. I wanna get to the rich bit. The real posh area."

"Where the celebrities live?" Ben smiles. "Guess you are a fame hunter."

"A girl can dream, right?"

They don't question the location any further as we stroll along. I bring Holly the whore to the fore and turn the conversation smutty, to keep their attention on what's to come.

I tell them what a dirty girl I am, who loves two at once, because I'm a hungry slut who can take it. East End Lucy-Lou doesn't have a filter. I giggle as I talk about loving a pounding in my ass, and sucking on dick like it's made of candy. I tell them how good I am at deepthroat, and how I can't wait to show them.

"You do threesomes often?" Ben asks. "You sound like a… pro."

Fuck. I thought he was going to say prostitute.

I shrug. "Had more threesomes than I can remember. Honestly, guys…" I grope my tits through my dress. "Having both tits sucked on at the same time is like dying and going to heaven."

"Fucking hell," Marcus says, eyeing my bulging cleavage, "I'm already hard and ready to blow."

Ben is nodding his approval – or agreement, licking his lips at the prospect.

And it works on me as well as them.

My pussy comes to life, sinking into the fantasy of what lies ahead. Of how good I'm going to be at living up to Heath's proposal. I do want two cocks. The fact that they belong to Ben and Marcus means fuck all to Holly. She wants it however she can get it.

My heart races when the outline of Heath's villa appears in the distance.

"Let's get on the sand," I say to the guys. "Do me a favour and help a girl out of her stilettos, will you? I wouldn't want to topple over."

Ben gets to his knees and unbuckles my designer shoes. I use the opportunity to show him I mean business, and hold his head to me, revealing my bare leg through the split in my dress.

His kisses are nothing but sweet little touches and it makes me giggle.

"I hope you do better than that when we're on the sand."

It rouses him. He grips my ass and presses his face to my crotch, rubbing his nose against my pussy through the satin.

Hmmm. He'll be ok. He'll cut it.

"Let's go!" I say, and take off barefoot, leaving the guys to chase me with my shoes in Ben's hand.

Fuck, how I run, with the sand between my toes as I get closer to Heath's villa.

"Come on!" I call, loving the pounding of the feet behind me as two men chase for the prize. A needy 'East End' slut with her holes on offer.

I could cry out in delight when I reach my destination, at the foot of Heath's grand villa wall. The beach is virtually private here – the splash of the waves down the shore a much better soundtrack than the thump of the bass in the club earlier. The breeze will carry the filthy grunts well.

I let out a satisfied moan when Marcus reaches me. He knocks me off my feet and sends my clutch flying, then wastes no time – pinning me on my back and grinding against me. I hitch up my legs and encourage him with a *yes*, showing the pair of them I'm for real.

I tug my satin dress down so they have access to my tits, my nipples hard in the sea air. The moon is bright overhead, and I can see both of the men's expressions changing – their lust coming to the fore.

This isn't just going to be a bit of slutty banter. This is for real.

"I meant it when I said I want to get pounded like a dirty fucking bitch," I tell them. "You better live up to it, or I'll have to walk back to the club to get some more."

"No fucking need to do that," Marcus says, still grinding on top of me. He slavers at my bare tits, his mouth popping as he sucks on my nipples, and Ben drops to his knees, unzipping his suit trousers to free his cock. My hand is straight to it, still gloved in satin, working his length.

He's alright. Decent enough. Nothing spectacular.

I'm glad that Heath demanded I take two.

Holly the whore is in her element now, consumed by the proposal. I beg Ben for his cock, opening my mouth like a hungry chick for him, and he leans down to give it to me. I slurp like a tramp, wet and gagging for it, hitching myself on the sand so Marcus can shimmy my dress up and pull my panties off.

"Lick my cunt," I say to him, slobbering around Ben's dick. "Get me ready for it."

Marcus doesn't know what he's doing with his tongue. *Lucy-Lou* would be disappointed, but luckily Holly isn't. Holly is a pro at getting what she needs.

I spread my legs on the sand and reach down to splay my pussy lips for him, angling myself towards his sweeping tongue. Yeah, he's got my clit. He's got it.

"Fingers," I tell him. "Get me ready."

He gives me one, tentatively. He's more of a pussy than my pussy, so I groan for him.

"More... oh fuck, I need more. Please. Way more than that."

The fucker shows me four before he plunges them deep.

I grunt and take it. Clearly I dented his pussy ego.

I like Marcus. I can feel a beast under the surface that hasn't yet had the chance to be tapped into. Poor guy is twenty-five tops, and likely never come across a girl like me.

"That's it," I tell him, my words blurred around Ben's cock. "Make me take it."

It feels good to have brutal fingers in my cunt, with a slobbery tongue lapping at my slit – no matter who it belongs to. I slow down with Ben's cock, as the last thing I want is a load of cum down my throat when we've barely even started.

"Your turn now," I say to Ben, smiling around his dick. "I want you to taste me, like I've tasted you."

He smiles down at me. "I'll gladly have a taste of your pussy, Lucy Lou. I'll eat you out all night long."

Marcus pulls away and Ben moves to take his place, but I scoot up and shake my head.

"No, let me ride you. I want to ride your fucking mouth."

Ben heeds my wish and lies on his back, not giving a shit for the sand on his suit. I straddle him, and lower my bare, sloppy cunt onto his open mouth, working my hips like I'm a rodeo rider, with my arms braced above his head.

I let the moans come naturally. I let my filthy words flow free as I tell them for real how much I like to be stretched, and used, and soiled like a whore. My big tits bob as I use Ben's mouth to get me high, and I tell Marcus I have rubbers in my discarded clutch so he can get his cock ready for me.

And then I look up at the villa.

It looks so familiar, even from this angle.

I wonder if Heath and Josh are watching me. I wonder if they can hear just how much of a slut I'm being with two unsuspecting men.

"Ready to take it?" Marcus says, his cock now sheathed.

I nod. "Desperate, more like it."

I dismount Ben's face, and position myself on all fours with my knees spread wide, my tits and ass on proud display, with my dress dishevelled. My submissive side shows its face, and I surrender to whatever is coming. I'm theirs now. They can do whatever they want with a whore like me.

"Use whatever holes you want," I groan. "Just fuck me."

Marcus isn't a pussy this time when it comes to my pussy. He slams my cunt in one, with his sheathed dick hitting right to the balls. The angle is out, but I don't care. I shunt against him and beg for harder. HARDER. I beg for Ben as well. MORE.

BOTH.

That's what I want.

Both of them.

They take it in turns at first – a couple of thrusts each in my pussy before they switch. Their timings get tighter as they get more desperate, and I encourage it.

"Don't worry," I say. "Plough me like the dirty bitch of your fantasies. Treat me like I'm a whore. I can take it."

I rub my clit, with my face in the sand as two random guys fuck my cunt, consumed by nothing more than offering everything I have for them. But I'm not doing it for them, I'm doing it for the men watching.

Because I know they are watching.

My boyfriend and my idol.

I can sense it.

It makes me tingle.

It gives me shivers.

It makes me come…

And it's when I'm coming that I ask the randoms fucking me for the obvious. Both of them at once, just like they knew I wanted.

They knew I wanted two guys at once, they just didn't know I meant it in one fucking hole…

"Sure," Ben says. "It'll be tight though, won't it? Don't you think it'll hurt?"

"Yeah." I smile. "It'll make my pussy hurt, but that will just make it better. Stretch my dirty fucking cunt like men, not weaklings."

"You really are a slut," Ben says.

Marcus says nothing.

Both guys are hesitating and I think I know why.

"Don't tell me," I say with an eye roll, "what if your cocks touch?"

"They will," Marcus finds his voice. "A spit roast would be better."

"Yeah," Ben says, "I like the sound of that."

Shit.

There's a big difference between experienced clients and guys out on the pull.

"You won't be touching, not really. You're wearing rubbers. This is a once in a lifetime opportunity, guys. I want both your cocks in my whore cunt, and I promise you the climax of your lives. Two rampant cocks banging one tight hole. You'll have bragging rights back home for ever."

"Good point," Ben says, working his sheathed cock. "Come on, Marcus, let's get her fucked."

Marcus is working his cock, too, but he's still hesitant.

"It works like this," I say, "You get on your back, I'll straddle you, get you nice and deep, then Ben comes in from behind, and before you know it, you're getting the fuck of your life."

"Yeah," Ben says, "get down on the sand, mate."

I get up on my feet, step up to Marcus, and touch my hands to his chest. "You get the added bonus of sucking my tits." A gentle shove and Marcus goes down.

Bingo!

I waste no time straddling him, grabbing his dick and sliding onto it, balls deep.

I lean forward, my tits dangling in Marcus's face, and look up at the villa walls as he grabs my tits and sucks a nipple into his mouth.

I smile up at *home*. At the men watching me. Because I've done it. I've given a performance as Holly that is true to my talents.

I picked the men Heath wanted, and got to the location he asked for, and I became the whore he wanted me to be. With strangers. All for him.

"Get ready," Ben says, dropping to the sand behind me. But I'm already there. My pussy wants the strain of taking two.

My cries are all real as two inexperienced guys try to double fuck me, because they haven't got the prowess or the skill of men used to the game, but that's ok. It's all ok. I grunt and grit my teeth, and I take it, two poor idiots with no cock knowledge slamming them right the way in.

My head is so far in the game now that I'm hedonistic.

When they're done with my pussy, they can take my ass, too. They can stretch my dirty hole like a pair of amateurs, and I'll wail at the sky all I need to.

I tell them so.

I tell the thrusting guys that I want them in my dirty fucking ass next, like a filthy bitch, and they speed up, cursing.

Ben and Marcus like this shit. They like it a lot.

I bet they are really fucking glad they met East End *Lucy-Lou* tonight.

Only Ben and Marcus won't be getting the chance.

A torchlight beams out like a beacon and lands on us, making me blink in the glare. I flinch as a voice booms loud.

"WHAT THE FUCK ARE YOU DOING?! GET THE FUCK AWAY! NOW!"

I know that voice really fucking well.

Oh my God.

It's Heath.

The glare blinds Marcus and Ben as much as it does me, and they pull out of my pussy with a *shit, shit, shit*. They push me aside like a ragdoll, so I sprawl in the sand, off balance. Such fucking gentlemen.

They scrabble to get their pants up and their dicks back in, and the pair of wimps fucking leg it. They sprint away back towards town, without a single scrap of care for *Lucy*, and the predicament she could be in.

Assholes.

Heath waits until they are shadows racing away before he reaches me and holds out a hand.

I brush the sand off myself as I get to my feet, and Josh is there with him, collecting my clutch and stilettos. Oh, and my panties. He gets them, too.

My heart pounds, trying to get a glimpse of their faces to see if I've passed the test.

"Well?" I ask them, aware of how damn flustered I sound. "I did it, right? Was I good enough? Did I deliver?"

"You did it, alright," Josh says and helps guide me towards the gate in the villa wall.

"And did you like it?" I ask the pair of them, stepping into the garden. "Was it fun?"

I can see the pair of them now, in the glow of the villa lighting. The familiarity makes my heart pang.

"No," Heath says, and wraps an arm around Josh's shoulder. "It wasn't fun at all, it was fucking shit, actually."

My world feels as though it's about to drop through the floor, but Josh leans in to kiss me.

"That was Heath's point, though," he tells me. "That was what it was all about. A test."

"What test?"

I feel so confused.

"Heath wanted to see *Holly* in action, with other men. And he wanted *me* to see Holly in action, with other men. He wanted to know what it felt like."

"You were a great performer, just as I knew you would be," Heath says, taking my hand. "But the experience wasn't the greatest. It was… interesting. Certainly interesting."

"Interesting?"

"It made Heath jealous," Josh tells me, landing a kiss on my shoulder.

My stomach lurches.

"Jealous? Really?!"

"Really," Heath says, opening the terrace door for me once we get to the pool. "And it made your boyfriend jealous, too."

I turn to Josh, my eyes searching his.

"It made you jealous? For real? What the hell?"

I can't stop staring at him as I back my way into the kitchen. I'm transfixed by his presence. By his demeanour. By the burn in his eyes.

The two amateurs' ferocity has nothing on the way my boyfriend takes hold of me and slams me onto the breakfast bar, positioning himself over me with a dirty scowl on his face.

"Yes, it made me jealous," he says. "Turns out watching something in the flesh is a tad bit different to hearing about it in the aftermath, Ella. You looked like a real fucking whore out there. Fuck, how you wanted them, that was no fucking act."

"I wanted *cock*, Josh, not *them*. They never meant shit to me. The proposal did."

I love the way his body feels against mine, just the way it should do.

"You're fucking mine," he says. "Even though you're a hooker, you belong to me. You know that? Those pricks thought they were lords of the fucking manor, but they're nothing. They were shit. This is the real deal, right here."

I tip my head back and nod.

"You don't need to tell me that, Josh. I already know. The real deal is right here, in this room. This is exactly where I belong. I belong to you."

I look over at the fire in Heath's eyes, so deep and brutal that it rivals Josh's.

And I know again there is something unspoken in the room...

I can feel what Heath wants to say, because I feel it myself. It thrums through me like electric waves.

I belong to him, too. That's the truth of it.

And not just me, either. The same applies to my boyfriend.

Yes, I belong to Josh, but I also belong to Heath Mason.

We both do.

Oh my God, we're fucked.

sixteen

I've never been on a yacht before, and have no idea whatsoever of the grandeur of one when it's up close and personal. It looks like a billionaire owns it, and they probably do. Heath is multi-millionaire turf, but even he raises his eyebrows when our host welcomes us onboard ready for our luxury afternoon tour of the Côte d'Azur.

The view from the deck is stunning, showing off the Vieux Port de Cannes and its bustling, high class atmosphere. It's so glamorous here that many *yacht* afternoons involve nothing more than hanging around on the boat while it's moored, but Heath has gone all out for this reward – as expected. We're going to be having a true sailing experience.

"I know you love the sea," he says.

He takes a seat next to me on the deck, not nearly so caught up in his disguise as he was at the vineyard just a few days ago. He's opted for casual. A designer shirt in whites and pale blues, with no tie. A dark blue pair of chino shorts finish it off perfectly. His hair is in a ponytail, and he's wearing a cap, but it isn't twisted up and out of view this time around, and his sunglasses are smaller today.

Josh is in purples, hardly a shocker. A deep mauve t-shirt with some black chino shorts like Heath's – clearly plucked out of Heath's wardrobe.

I'm the only one truly dressed up for the occasion, my makeup styled to the max and my hair flowing down my back, sleek and straight. I'm in a fitted black sundress, with my tiny black bikini underneath, and it barely covers my ass.

I adore the way the guys don't take their eyes away from me for so much as a second. The possessiveness in the air from last night still lingers, tense. Hot. Spicy. Enough to give me tingles.

These two stunning men haven't stopped staring at me all morning. Even through our fruit salad breakfast they looked more ready to eat me than their slices of watermelon. They'd have been more than welcome to, if we hadn't been pushed to get ready for our adventure.

"Drinks, Mr Mason?" our assistant asks Heath, clearly recognising him, but Heath directs the question to me. "Le souhait de la dame vient en premier." *Ladies first.*

"An orange juice, please," I say. "I've still got a muggy head from all those cocktails last night."

"Same," Josh says. "Add some lemonade to mine though, please."

Heath is grinning, his smile perfect in the sunlight. "In that case, I'll side with these conservative sailors and go for a juice myself. I'll have grapefruit, please. Grapefruit and soda."

The assistant leaves us to it, and I dare to probe Heath as to the prices on here, even for an orange juice.

"You don't want to know," he says. "It's quite frankly ridiculous, but that's Cannes for you. I bought a place here when I was stupid enough to think I wanted to be at the heart of the faux, pretentious celebrity community, but the villa became too much of a home to let go."

"Woah. We must have cost you a fortune on our excursions this week."

Heath is still smiling, kicking his legs out with ease. "You make it an entirely different matter altogether. You make the experience more than worth it. I've enjoyed every single second. Money well spent." He looks at me in particular. "I wouldn't deny you anything, Ella. Any capital involved is irrelevant."

"Neither would I," Josh adds, then elbows Heath in the arm. "Heathy baby may have all the dollar and swagger of an A Lister, but I'd still pamper you like a fucking princess."

"You *do* pamper me like a fucking princess," I say to my boyfriend, leaning over to plant a kiss on his cheek. "Every single day. And you know what they say? Treat me like a princess, fuck me like a whore. I'm a winner on both fronts."

"Thumbs up for that," Heath says. "And I'm not a bloody A Lister, Josh, thank God. I can't hack the attention of being a B Lister, let alone the top of the tree."

Heath is playing it down a bit. Yeah, worldwide he has more of a cult status than a mega movie celeb would have, but in London, he's one of the best known faces on TV.

I think he's playing it down for himself, more than anyone else right now, and that works for me. Whatever it takes to make him feel good. He's certainly feeling better at being outside the villa walls.

I just hope it can last when we're gone.

When we're gone.

Fuck, how that thought pains.

Tomorrow morning we'll be on a flight out of here, back to not-so-sunny Heathrow airport.

It's not just the hangover giving me nausea, it's the knowledge that we'll be leaving our wonderful client behind. So much of me wants to take him by the hand and ask him to come with us, but I can't. I daren't.

Nausea turns into excitement as the yacht's engine fires up. I hand my juice to Josh so that I can jump up and down as we depart from the marina, transfixed by the trail of foam the boat is leaving behind.

I love the sea. It's AMAZING. I love being ON the sea. It's absolutely out of this fucking world.

Heath dismisses our assistant with a *non, non, merci* when they offer us a talk as to what the tour involves. Turns out he already knows the deal well enough himself.

We are headed for the Lérins Islands. A group of five Mediterranean islands located off the coast of Cannes. The two largest islands are Île Sainte-Marguerite and Île Saint-Honorat apparently, but there are some smaller ones that are uninhabited. Jesus, every single view is spectacular.

We have the opportunity to moor up and explore the islands if we want to, but I have to decline. I don't want to get off the sea. I don't want to leave this gorgeous boat, not even for a second.

"Sorry," I say. "I'm getting cheeky. I just… I love it."

"That's ok, curva," Heath tells me. "If you would prefer to stay on the boat, we'll stay on the boat."

"I love the idea of the islands," I say. "There are a billion things I'd like to explore here, I just… this is so great being on here. With you."

"Why, thank you." Heath slaps Josh's leg playfully. "And how about you, sweet Joshua? Are you happy staying on the boat?"

"Too right," Josh says. "This is a beast of a trip already without parking up anywhere."

"Maybe next time, though?" I say, hopefully, praying there will be a next time here with Heath, because if there isn't…

My heart can't even go there.

Heath grins at me. "We'll do a proper trip of the islands another time, don't worry. For now, let's all just enjoy the sea."

His words are like music to my soul, and from the way Josh is grinning out at the waves, they are music to his, too. All three of us are buzzing high – and the hangover recovery begins. My soul loosens along with the tension in my head, and my stomach stops turning. No seasickness for me.

I adore the yacht, with its rich interior, but I barely spend any time in it. Fuck the cinema room – which is considerably bigger than Heath's, and fuck the bar and the games room, too. I want to be Rose on the Titanic, standing with my arms spread at the guard rail and letting the wind of the ocean sweep my heart into the clouds.

"I think you must have been a mermaid in a past life," Josh says when I plop my butt down between them after another squeak and arm spread. "A sea addict."

"Good job I have a villa in Cannes, isn't it?" Heath says, and it's a rhetorical question, half spoken in jest, but it cements something.

He wants us back here. For real.

I could cry with glee, I'm so happy.

It turns out that three hours on a yacht feels like sweet FA once it's over. I could spend three years on one, quite happily, and I look at the boat wistfully as we depart. I figure we'll get a cab straight back home and disappear into the secluded confines of the villa, but Heath hangs back at the dock.

"Wait one moment. Maybe we could sample one of the seafront bars?" he says. "It's been a while since I frequented one."

My eyes widen. A bar? Right here on the bustling seafront? Heath really has picked up his socialising game.

"Sure thing, of course," I say, and Josh nods.

"Whatever you want, *boss*."

The bar Heath is gesturing to is heaving, and clearly mega elite. Swathes of swanky guys in white shirts and shorts. Youngsters blatantly from wealth, hitting it with the loud banter. Women who look straight out of Vogue.

I feel a bit out of my depth with this place, even though I'm lucky enough to be adept at playing extroverted, so I feel a twinge for poor introverted Heath, but he strides ahead. Josh meets me with a smirk as I look his way.

"He's coming out of his shell. It's fantastic. Look at the grin on his face."

"Think people will recognise him?"

Josh takes my hand as we follow our client towards the entrance.

"I'd imagine so. I mean, his hat does a semi decent job and sunglasses are sunglasses, but he's Heath. People know Heath Mason. They'll recognise his hair, even if they can't pin him down for absolute certain."

We're at the entrance when two girls come racing past us, shrieking about a real A Lister being in the bar and summoning their friends via video call.

Josh smiles at that.

"Actually, maybe he'll be alright. There are plenty of eyes on plenty of people, it seems. He might just be able to shrink into the sea of posh without causing a stir."

Heath is beckoning us over, and it gives me another damn round of butterflies to see how excited he is when the staff offer us a booth in the central aisle. We're amidst the elite hustle and bustle, and Heath is glowing as the server hands us all a copy of the bar menu. The menu is as lavish as the rest of the place – cut into the shape of the Gates of Glory – foiled in gold.

Fuck seasickness, it's *price* sickness that almost has me barfing when I scan the drinks list.

Fifty thousand fucking dollars a pop for a bottle of some crazy ass champagne?! Literally. For one pop and about five glasses. This place has to be having a fucking laugh!

Even the cheapest bottle on this menu costs thousands. Five hundred a pop for a cocktail last night was mental enough, but ten grand for a bottle of champers? Base rate? It feels too much. Way too much.

"What would you like?" Heath asks, with his easy grin still bright on his face.

"Maybe another orange juice, please."

He tips his head, laughing. "An orange juice, in this place? Don't you fancy some champagne?"

I actually feel sick at the thought of fifty thousand for one fucking bottle.

"I think I'm alright for champagne, thanks," I say, wincing as I point to my head. "Still a bit muggy."

"You don't need to have champagne," Heath says. "You could have a spritzer? A cocktail? Bucks fizz? There are plenty of your favourite sparkling wines on here, too. Take a look."

Bizarrely, I don't want to take a look. Being on a yacht with Heath Mason earlier felt elite beyond elite, and so did the club and restaurant last night – before I turned into a beach slut, but something feels off about this place.

The atmosphere is… different.

I realise to my absolute horror that I don't like it. I don't like it at all.

Here, in this bustling show off den, I get another foul taste of what the celebrity culture can be like. Competitive and snarky. Judgemental. Ugly and social media driven, everyone out to prove something. Because that's what the atmosphere is in here. Snobby.

Snobby and elitist and shallow as fuck.

I don't know how such a glamourous place could give me the heebies, but it does. It feels septic.

"You alright?" Josh asks, putting down his drinks menu to squeeze my knee. "You got the after effects of being on the sea or something?"

I shake my head. "No, no. I'm alright." I try to focus on the menu. This is all about Heath's happiness and experience. Not mine. "Maybe I should go for a lovely sparkling white…"

The words on the list blur as I scan them, the insane prices stabbing me in the guts. I should expect this. The more glamorous the location, the higher the prices, right? The Agency is no different. You get what you pay for. You want elite service, you pay elite prices for them.

I take a breath, because I'm ok with that. If people can afford it, and want to enjoy it, then that's how it is. If Heath can afford to treat us, and treat himself, and he wants to, then that's cool.

Or it is until a group to the side of us get a server arriving at their table with six bottles of the fifty grand champagne in a huge bucket, brimming with ice.

Three hundred grand's worth of champagne in one fucking bucket.

The guys at the table are youngsters, barely my age. They let out Etonian rich boy type *huzzahs*, practically snorting like toff nosed pricks, and the hairs on the back of my neck prickle.

"Fucking hell," Josh says. "They're really going for it, getting sloshed at fifty grand a bottle."

Heath's eyes narrow as he looks at them, but he doesn't comment, just watches. Like the rest of the place. The twats suddenly get the attention of the whole damn bar when one of the idiots stands up and raises a bottle over his head.

"Water fight!" he yells, and his friends cheer along, grabbing a bottle of champagne each and raising them over their heads like snobby bully boys.

Water fight? What the fuck? Surely not…

The pig-headed jackasses shake the bottles of fifty grand champagne with everything they've got, practically wanking the bottles in their desperation to get the fizz pumped. Time slows down as I watch them. The smug expressions on their spoiled ass faces, their sheer delight at having more money than brains.

The first cork gets popped, and the rest fire in quick succession, and it's for fucking real. It's a water fight – or a champagne fight to be specific. Like dumbass kids in a school yard.

The idiot pricks use those prized bottles of deluxe, world class champagne as fire hoses to soak the shit out of each other, laughing like pre-schoolers as they do it. Three hundred thousand fucking pounds spewing over each other without a care.

It transports me back to the Ella working every hour she could at minimum wage, just to feed herself on pasta through the month and pay the bills. The Ella who avoided the tube to save the fare, even though her feet were killing her after twelve hours straight on her feet already. I remember the fear and dread at checking my account balance, and realising I only had a few pounds left until my next pay day – crying because I couldn't book in any more shifts, I was working so many already. I used to be so fucking scared.

And that Ella sees these idiots through one sorry lens.

They aren't just smug idiots, out to show off their wealth to the world.

They are cunts.

Selfish. Entitled. Stuck up, snotty cunts, who don't give a fuck about anything but their own bloated egos.

It stabs a knife into a buried wound, skewering straight into my guts.

I'm no longer the entertainer Holly when I get to my feet at the table and shoot them a look that could kill. I walk towards them, one step at a time, shaking Josh's hand off as he reaches for mine.

It takes the idiots a few seconds to notice my approach, wet shirted and laughing their heads off as they summon a waiter for another six bottles.

"Makes you feel good, does it?" I ask the ringleader. "Throwing cash around like it's worth nothing whatsoever, just for a pathetic ego boost? People are starving. Homeless. Battling to earn enough money to pay for their families to eat every month, and you lot… you're a fucking disgrace. A joke."

Rage flows through my arms so strongly, I have to clench my fists at my side.

One of the guys looks at me like I'm shit on his shoe.

"Oh, woe is me, says you, in fucking Cannes, you snotty bitch." Then he laughs. "Oh wait, are you not upper class? Seems not from your accent. Are you a whore on someone's arm? I bet your pussy is worth less than one of these bottles, so why don't you shut your self-righteous mouth and quit complaining?"

One of his friends laughs along with him.

"You've got it nailed, Jimmy. She's definitely a hooker, look at her." He pauses. "How about we give you a bottle and you come sit at our table instead? Let's fill your trappy mouth up with something other than envy."

I feel winded, because the burn inside me is anything but envy.

It's pain.

Hurt.

"You're nothing but entitled, greedy fuckups," I say. "Every fucking one of you. You're fucking disgusting."

I don't know where I'm dashing to when I've had my say, I just go. Every pair of eyes in the place burn in my direction, but I can't control myself. All I can think of is the bullying bitches where I used to work, despising me and judging me, and making me take the blame for all their poor efforts and fuckups, just because I was desperate.

Nothing is any different here amongst this kind of *elite*. This place is full of wankers.

I hear Josh's voice booming in the background, but I can't bear to face him right now. My throat is choked up with the need to cry, which is stupid. I'm at the happiest point in my whole fucking life, but some rivers run deep. The memory of hopelessness is still strong enough to bury me.

One of the servers opens the barrier entrance for me and I dash on down to the marina. People are staring, I feel them in a blur, but I keep walking, breathing as deep as I can so I don't break and cry, because what the fuck have I just done? And what the fuck am I fucking doing?!

I'm not Ella here. I'm Holly the whore. I *should* be Holly the whore, and Holly has no right to be drawing attention to Heath or acting like that in any circumstances. I've fucked up big time.

"Ella!"

Oh hell, I hear Heath's voice in the distance, and I stop walking, trying to compose myself.

"Ella, wait! Stop!"

I try to bury the pain, and focus on the apology, because I owe him one. I should be grovelling on my knees for being so fucking unprofessional after all he's done, and he's got every right to be fuming at me.

I turn to face him, and manage a *sorry* before my breaths choke me up. I don't have any words other than that, feeling so small and pathetic and vulnerable and *wrong* that I don't know where to start.

"Breathe," Heath says, and his voice is so still. No rage there at all.

"Leave," I manage to whimper. "Get away from me, before anyone sees you. I'm sorry. I'm really, really fucking sorry. I just... I can't..."

I feel the faces all around us, watching. I know how close he is, stepping forward.

"Leave!" I hiss. "Honestly, Heath, just go. Go! I'm so sorry."

But Heath Mason shakes his head. He takes off his sunglasses, so his blue eyes lock onto mine, and tosses his cap on the floor.

He's him.

And he's coming towards me.

"I'm sorry," I try again, but he tells me to *shh* – his beautiful eyes so warm, and that's when the tears finally fall.

"You have nothing to be sorry for," he says. "Everything you said is true. And I admire you for it. Ella, I admire you, full stop."

His words thump my ribs, making my heart pang.

"I shouldn't have done that..."

He brushes his thumb across my cheek, wiping a tear away.

"Everyone *should* have. Those idiots deserve every word they got, and you deserve this."

I stiffen up as he lands his gorgeous lips on mine, because he has to be fucking crazy. He's lost his mind, kissing me without his sunglasses on while people watch us. People who will know who he is.

Except I can't stay stiff in his arms with his mouth on mine. I can't fight the way I want him, wrapping my arms around his shoulders and kissing him back as my tears keep on falling.

"I'm proud of you," he says when he pulls away. "I'm proud of everything you are, and you should be, too."

I have no words, only the blooming feeling of raw emotion.

Love.

I flinch as I hear the pounding of feet heading in our direction, but it's Josh, racing towards us at full pelt.

"Let's get the fuck out of here," he says, catching his breath. "I just threw that guy over the railings, and tripped his gobby mate up in the aisle."

"You did what?!" My eyes widen, but his cheeky smirk shines bright.

"They fucking deserved it," my boyfriend says. "Nobody calls my princess a trappy hooker."

"*Our* princess," Heath corrects him. "Good for you, Josh."

Thank fuck there are a bank of cabs waiting at the top of the marina driveway, because my adrenaline spike eases away to nothing and leaves me like a shell.

I need *home*.

The villa, with its high walls, its secluded grounds, and its beautiful silence.

And my two princes there to share it with.

eighteen

SATURDAY

Tonight, there will be no proposal.
Just us. Making love.

Wow, ok. Not what I was expecting.

The proposal takes me aback. And I want to be sure... I *need* to be sure...

This is another one of Heath's freshly drawn up revisions. Different kind of pen and paper, like the one last night. I hold it in my hands, re-reading his cursive handwriting, fascinated by the sentiment in his words.

Just us. Making love.

I pass the piece of paper to Josh so he can see Heath's scrawl for himself.

"No proposal? Really?" I ask our client.

"No, no proposal. Not tonight."

"There were seven envelopes originally, and this one definitely wasn't amongst the stack you were holding up on night one."

"That's correct. It wasn't."

I get a flash of guilt.

"Are you sure this is what you want? If you're trying to go gentle with me because I got upset earlier, you don't need to. I'm ok now. I'm fine, I promise."

The look in Heath's eyes knocks me back, the pale blue of his irises so raw.

"I'm positive it's what I want. I've never been so sure of a proposal in my life."

Josh is silent as he holds the paper. It's not like him to be lost for words, but he doesn't speak, just nods. Slowly.

He must be feeling the sentiment, just like I am. So much power in such few words.

He folds up the proposal and puts it back in the envelope, placing it between the three of us on the coffee table.

I've performed plenty of proposals as Holly the whore by now, packed full of hardcore, or roleplay, or specific kinks and desires. But making love?

The butterflies are so fierce, they're like palpitations.

"How about you, Ella? Are you ok with that?" Heath asks.

I feel churned up by just how much it means.

Or could mean.

Fucking hell.

"I'm more than ok with that. It'll be amazing."

"And you, Josh?" Heath says. "Are you ok with it?"

My stomach ties itself in glorious knots when I see the conviction in Josh's eyes.

"Have to agree with Ells," he says. "It sounds… incredible."

Silence.

Heavy, beautiful silence. Like thick orange clouds on a sunset sky.

Heath's smile breaks the tension.

"Good. But first, I have things planned. A lovely farewell surprise before my sweet curvas wave their goodbyes in the morning."

His smirk of a smile shows the irony. Curvas... sure.

"Come," he says. "Our meal should be arriving soon."

"You've got us a takeout?" Josh asks as we follow our host through the villa to the dining suite.

"A tad more upmarket than a pizza delivery with a side of fries, but yes, it's a takeout. It's being delivered from a bistro in town. Coq au Vin, Beef Bourguignon and Sole Meunière. With some additional sides, of course. I thought we could share a platter."

I help Josh set the dining table while Heath disappears to prepare the wine. We share a look as we lay the cutlery, and my heart bleeds for my boyfriend. Heath's simple words have touched deep, that much is clear.

"Has he ever asked you to make love before?" I whisper, and Josh shakes his head.

"Not like that, no."

I give him a gentle smile.

"It's amazing," I say. "This whole thing has been amazing."

"I know. So *amazing* that things will never be the same again."

"Would you want them to be?" My heart thumps as he lays out the last of the spoons.

"No. Would you?"

The smile is still on my face.

"No."

Josh braces himself on the tabletop.

"I don't know where things are gonna go from here though, Ells, seriously. What can we do? Heath's a client. We're hookers, bound by Agency standards. And even if we weren't, Heath's never going to want this in the spotlight. Not in a thousand years. Even visiting us in Belgravia would freak the fuck out of him, terrified the press would be snapping at his heels. He hates it."

I hold up a hand, with a *shhh*.

"Don't worry about it yet. We'll figure it out. Until then, we just enjoy it. All three of us, together."

He lets out a sigh.

"You sound more like me than I do myself." He shakes his concerns away. "You're right. Let's just enjoy it. All three of us, together."

As it should be. That's what I want to say.

This isn't Weston the entertainer talking to me, any more than it's Holly the hardcorer talking to him. We're just us. Like Heath wanted it.

Ella and Josh.

Truth be known, we've been Ella and Josh since we first pulled up in the driveway.

I'm glad to hear Heath's footsteps approach from the kitchen area, as I could do with some drink to get me underway. I turn to face our host as he arrives, expecting wine bottles and glasses, but instead he has a tray of candles. Three of them. Solid white pillars, with flecks of rose petals, lined up on slate.

He places the slate on the table and lights one candle before handing the lighter to me, and it's like a scene from Nighttime Whispers. The fated love of The Count and Polly Anna…

Bloody hell, this is getting deep.

Josh takes the lighter next and lights his.

Three flames.

Three lovers.

One night left.

I'm going to give my all to making the most of it.

"All set for a lovely meal?" Heath asks, as Josh and I stare at the flickering flames.

As if on cue, the bell sounds out from the main gate, and Heath heads off to collect our food. I wonder if Josh is going to voice anything more to me about what lies ahead or suggest how things could pan out, but he doesn't. He seems to have pushed his trepidation aside for now – back to the usual Joshua. He has a spring in his step as he walks over to pick up the wine tray.

Jeez, Heath has gone all out with the meal choices. I've never tried Sole Meunière before, but it's absolutely delicious. I munch away as we split the dishes, and the conversation flows between us like it always does. We laugh about how Heath first introduced Josh to mussels several years back, and how our vampire lover had never seen anyone so edgy with a fork in his life.

"They looked weird as fuck, to be fair," Josh says. "I've had them in restaurants since, but seriously, Heath. With your wacko dining set they looked like mini demons from the Little Shop of Horrors."

Heath pats his lips with his napkin, looking at me.

"He's exaggerating."

"No, I'm not! Get that dinner set out next time we're at yours and serve them to Ella. She can be the judge."

"He's talking about a green cauldron serving bowl," Heath tells me. "And they were in a broth."

"Hiding in the depths like mini demons, yes."

"You enjoyed them!"

"I was pretending."

"That's the biggest pile of crap I've ever heard. I can read you like a book, Josh. You loved the demonic bastards. And you fucking know it."

Fucking hell, the spark between these two guys in the candlelight is beautiful. The way they match each other's smiles, eyebrows so alive as they chat together. And their eyes so attentive when they bring me into the conversation along with them.

One day I only pray I know Heath as well as Josh does. I've only just scratched the surface, and he's consumed me.

We have ice cream for dessert, relaxing on the terrace as the sun dips down on the horizon. I look out over the infinity pool, and remember how overwhelmed I was by Heath's haven when we first showed up here. I never believed it would feel like home.

But home is where Heath is, as well as Josh. That's at the heart of it.

I want some time to get ready for our 'non-proposal', so I let the guys know I have a surprise of my own I want to share with them. It's one piece of evening lingerie I haven't revealed yet, and it will fit the bill just right.

I reach Heath's bedroom and flick on the lights, casting my eyes over the massive bed taking centre stage. I've never slept so well in my life as I have since I've been here. With its deluxe sheets and its cloudlike mattress, it's the perfect canvas for lovemaking. It's this spot I'll be coaxing the guys into later.

I have my bedtime outfit stashed in my case. It's a perfect contrast to my uber goth makeup and my long black hair. A babydoll that looks almost virginal – in pure white lace, with white satin panties, that tie up at either side with a bow.

I touch up my makeup before I get dressed, ensuring that my contouring and lashes are on point after my crying fit earlier. I want to look as fine as possible for the beautiful Heath Mason and my stunner of a boyfriend.

I tie the sides of my panties up, and rub my fingers up and down my slit through the satin. It clings nice and tightly. The cups of the babydoll work a treat to hitch my tits up, and the lace glides down my ribs, long enough to reach the top of my thighs.

It's a strange sensation, looking at myself in the mirror and giving myself a twirl. I'm usually psyched up for a proposal laid out, not laid bare emotionally, with two men I adore.

"Hey, guys," I say when I arrive back at the terrace, and they both twist around on their loungers.

Their expressions are a picture. Josh holds his hand up to Heath for a high five.

"That's a new outfit," my boyfriend says to me.

"Yes, it is. I was saving it."

"Good choice. You look incredible."

"Thank you."

He knows me well enough to read how my energy has changed

since disappearing into the bedroom. I've still got a smile on my face, yeah, but my body is needy under the lace. Craving contact. Craving sex. Craving *them*.

He can see it in my eyes. Just like I can see it in his.

I walk between their loungers and stand with my back to the pool, facing the pair of them. My two lovers.

It's Heath's lap I drop onto, trailing my fingers up Josh's leg on the way over. Heath's still in his blue and white shirt from earlier, and I brush my lips against his as I begin to unbutton it.

"You're so fucking beautiful, Ella," he says.

"So are you."

His hand wraps around the back of my neck and holds me close as his lips press to mine. The kiss is slow, deep, sensual… his tongue savouring the taste while I free his chest from his shirt. I run my hands down his ripped abs, grinding my palms against his crotch just a touch, so I can feel the length of him, swollen proud.

I close my eyes and soak into the atmosphere.

Crazy.

Surreal.

Me and Heath Mason, in the evening sun.

Making love.

We're not a twosome for long. I hear Josh's lounger move, and within a moment he lands a kiss on my cheek. That's enough of a knock at the door for Heath to turn his head and welcome him into the kiss with us. A three-way of tongues, entwined. Wet and wanting.

Josh's pierced tongue feels amazing as it sweeps and dances…

Maybe one day Heath will follow suit and get one – just like he did with the others.

I unbutton Josh's shirt as we kiss, and he shrugs it from his shoulders. His muscles are tighter than Heath's but it's a close call. I run my hands up and down their magnificent chests.

There's a primal side to me knocking at my own internal door, wanting to be pinned and slammed and ravaged by these hot men and their rampant cocks. I'm so used to bouncing, and begging, and spilling filth from my scarlet lips that the gentle silence of the three of us makes me a tad nervous. There is no mask to hide behind, and no slut to unleash to a format. No Holly the whore, ready to grab the fix of pleasure at any cost.

"You're so beautiful, baby," Josh says, between kisses, and I'm not sure if it's me or Heath he's talking to, but it doesn't make any difference. The sentiment would be the same.

"Can we go to the bedroom, guys?" I ask. "I want to be in bed with both of you, floating on cloud nine."

"Good analogy," Heath says, his cock like a pole as he shifts underneath me on the lounger. "Let's go. Tonight, the bedroom is where we belong."

The guys discard their shirts and chinos on the way through the villa – the three of us still tangled in kisses all the way as they undress. I'm fully made up in my babydoll, the white lace intact when Heath lifts me up in the bedroom to drop me on the bed.

It's such a huge mattress that I scoot to get in the middle, and they climb up along with me, one on either side. Fuck, how I'm spoiled by their caresses. Teased by the tips of their fingers as their mouths focus on mine.

Again, my inner slut wants to beg for it, but again, I quieten the voice. Instead, I murmur, savouring every kiss and every touch, letting my inner emotions bloom. Heath kisses my neck, nipping gently, but there is no ferocity in his teeth tonight. I'm not a victim of The Count's savagery. Josh trails his lips across my collarbone, then down... lower. His breaths are hot against my exposed cleavage, my nipples straining inside my babydoll, desperate for touch. For heat. For *him*.

"Such a gorgeous outfit," he says. "It's almost a shame to take you out of it. *Almost.*"

He tugs down the lace so tenderly that my bullet nipple pops free like a jack-in-the-box. He groans as he sucks it into his mouth, and so do I – the ball of his tongue piercing sending tingles right the way down to my clit. The guys ease my legs open, one thigh each, but they don't touch my pussy, just hold me there in position. Heath pulls down the other side of my babydoll, and takes my other nipple into his mouth, and I'm sucked by the pair of them at once, holding their heads to me as I smile up at the ceiling. I run my fingers through Heath's silky hair, and tickle the back of Josh's neck in appreciation. I arch and squirm, riding invisible waves of need, but their hands stay on my thighs and not my pussy. *Teases.* I go along at the natural pace for once. I feel their cocks, hard against my sides, but I don't reach down to touch them – just take it slowly. So, so slowly.

They feast on my tits with their horny mouths, and the pressure in me builds, my clit sparking.

"Please..." I say. "Make me come. I want to come for you."

The two men don't so much as undo the bows on my panties. Josh simply trails his fingers up and down my clammy slit through the satin, and presses his mouth to my ear.

"Gently," he says. "It's going to be such a beautiful temptation, baby. So beautiful."

The rhythm with which he strokes my slit is so slow, it's almost torturous. I'm delirious, high on endorphins as he brings me to the peak and then eases me off, over and over. He's too skilled to battle with. He knows how to pull my strings far too well for that.

"Your turn," he says to Heath, and Heath takes over – his long vampiric fingers pressing just a touch harder against my slit as he works me.

My pussy is calling out for a slamming, and I'd usually be a slut between this pair – begging to be stretched, stretched, stretched and fucking ravaged. But this is the other side of the spectrum. So soft and caring.

I revel in the sensation, looking deep into Heath's ice-cool eyes as he brings me to the edge.

He's never seen me like this before. Not like Josh has.

I pull my gorgeous idol in for another kiss, moaning against his mouth as he eases me over the edge and lets me come for him. And again, it's an amazing first, coming against his fingers as he continues to kiss me.

Josh kisses Heath's neck as the two of us play, telling us how fucking good it feels to share such highs together.

I'm still flying high when the guys pull the ribbons of my panties loose and tug the satin clear. My clit is still so tender to the touch that I flinch when Josh splays the butterfly – but he doesn't push me for more, just gets up close and blows hot breath on the easing flame.

"I want to watch Heath make love to you," he says, and turns to our other lover. "Heathy baby, fuck Ella nice and slow. Fuck her like you love her."

"That won't be hard," Heath says, looking me in the eyes. "Since I do. I do love Ella." He lands a kiss on Josh's lips. "Just like I love you."

It feels like I've been sucker punched with raw emotion. *Love.* Spoken aloud.

I'm jaw-dropped.

I'm tongue-tied.

I'm fucking speechless and I'm sure I could faint if I tried.

"Sweet Ella," Heath says and it feels so natural when he climbs on top of me.

My pussy is aching for his cock when he eases the head in, and my lips are desperate for more of his. For more kissing. I could never get enough.

It makes my heart flutter in the most twisty of ways to make love to another man in front of my boyfriend. We're on a three-way street where every line is now blurred and truly fucking blissful.

Heath's barbells are a slow torment as he sinks them into me, one by one. I whimper into his kisses, and his tongue swirls match the circle of his hips as he works his way into me. A perfect tandem of sensations.

"You two look so fucking good together," Josh says. "I love it. And I need to feel the love, too." He bends down to kiss Heath's ear. "Can I make love to you while you make love to my girlfriend?"

Heath nods as we kiss, and my pussy tightens around his cock.

Josh is going to fuck Heath's ass, while Heath fucks me. Oh yes, oh fucking yes…

There is no driving in hard this time when it comes to Josh and Heath, though. No slammers, or thrusts or savagery. Heath is still fucking me deep and slow when I hear the squelch of lube behind him. Heath moans into my mouth as Josh positions himself at his rear, and his muscles tense with every pop as Josh's cock inches its way in.

Fucking in sync comes so naturally between us, it's like we were born for it.

Heath impales me deep and slow as I urge him on, then backs onto Josh's invading cock every time he pulls away. I watch Josh kissing Heath's shoulder from behind, smiling up at him as he whispers loving words into his ear, and I'm right there with them, feeling every flutter of romance myself.

We ride the waves, like the sea lapping at the shore until the tide comes in. Building and building, but revelling in every touching moment…

Because there is no doubt about it now. Not with this kind of energy in the room.

This is what Heath meant when he scrawled those words on the paper earlier. He meant this.

This is love making.

Exactly this.

And I'm so glad he fucking wrote it.

No matter what tomorrow morning brings, I'm so fucking glad he wrote it.

We come together in a perfect trio, and breathe together in the aftermath, holding each other tight. If we weren't so pushed for time, I'd sleep in their arms all night long, but every moment is precious. I kiss the guys as they fuck each other into the night, and they kiss each other as each of them takes a turn with me.

We fuck, we suck, we kiss, and we come. But most of all, we *feel*.

Love. What a beautiful thing.

By the time the morning comes, we're still a tangle of limbs and hungry kisses. I feel my soul sinking, because I don't want to let this go.

I don't want to catch the plane, and I don't want to say goodbye to Heath.

I don't want to leave the bubble of us we've built here, in a glorious villa in Cannes.

The clock is not kind. The minutes tick by in a flash as Josh and I pack up our belongings together, with Heath looking on. The connection is still thrumming, strong. And it only makes it harder.

When Heath disappears into the kitchen to prep some fruit salad for breakfast, I take Josh by the arm and pull him close.

"Can we ask to stay longer? Shall we ask him to come back with us? What do we do now? Are we really going to just drive away?"

Josh looks as broken by the thought as I do, but he pastes on a smile.

"I've been doing this for years, Ells. Leaving him behind. Cannes, with three of us involved, is a whole other league, but loving Heath and leaving Heath I'm familiar with. It's different now, and it always will be, but we need to give it time. All of us. We have clients, and he has a production to prepare for."

"I don't give a fuck about any of that right now. I just want us here with him."

I feel myself choking up, even though it was Josh freaking out last night, not me.

"Morning after syndrome," my boyfriend says, and runs a thumb across my cheek.

"*Life* after syndrome more like it."

"Yeah, I get you. I'm there, too. But we need to do it, Ella. Life goes on, and Heath will be in it with us. We just need to figure out how."

"And when, and where, and how often…"

"Yeah, many questions. But we'll do it. He wants it as much as we do."

I've no doubt whatsoever about that.

Heath has the same energy of despondency himself when we wheel our cases into the breakfast room. He has coffee and juices and a whole platter of fruit prepped, and a glowing smile on his face, but there is more to it than that.

I guess that once the connection of soul energy has been tapped into, the instincts won't be ignored. And mine are fucking screaming.

"I'll miss you," he says, like it needs pointing out.

"No shit," I reply. "We'll be missing you like hell until we see you next."

"Morning after syndrome doesn't even come close," Josh adds, and the three of us toast with an orange juice, trying our best to keep our humour as we eat our breakfast.

"You'd better have these back," Heath says, and returns our passports and phones from the security safe. My God, it feels so long ago that we handed them over.

I stare at my blank handset. I've become so used to being disconnected from the world.

Heath checks the time.

"Your cab will be here soon, so you should probably get out there. We should say our goodbyes in here. You know, because of..."

"Privacy, yeah, I know," I say for him.

"Privacy at all costs, yeah, cool," Josh says. "Come here."

He pulls the two of us into his arms, and it's a warmth I don't want to leave. I don't want to break away, and I don't want to say goodbye, and I don't want to be waiting outside like two random tourists when a cab pulls up to whisk us away, but what will be will be.

We kiss in a long, desperate whirlwind – once, twice, three times on the way to the front door, kisses and *goodbyes* and *see you soons* and... *love you!*

And then the door is closed behind us.

Josh and I don't bother speaking. We're just standing alone in the morning heat together when the driveway gates open and the cab rolls in. We load our stuff into the back, trying to act like things are normal and dandy, even though my ribs feel speared with the loss at what, or rather, *who*, we are leaving behind.

I figure we've got this. Deep breaths. Pasted on smiles. Everything under control.

No big deal, no big deal, no big deal...

"We'll be seeing him again soon, baby," Josh whispers, right into my ear. "Real soon. As soon as we can. We'll make it work, and we'll keep it under wraps. We'll make it happen. Somehow."

I nod, mute as I slide into the backseat. I get a stabbing pain in my gut when the taxi pulls away, because here we are, on our way back to the airport. Our Naughty Week is over, and our lover has been left behind.

I can't help the silent tears that fall from my eyes. I wipe them away with swats of my hand so the driver doesn't see them, and I don't look at Josh. I can't.

I know he's battling with tears of his own.

epilogue

The car zooms along towards the airport, and I'm desperate to tell the cab driver to turn around and take us back to Heath's place, it hurts so fucking bad. This isn't morning after syndrome, and it isn't *week* after syndrome – it's leaving someone you're in love with behind, not knowing when the hell you'll see them again. The driver has the radio on, playing some upbeat pop without a care in the world, swaying his head from side to side. Lucky bastard.

"It'll be alright," Josh tells me in the backseat. "Proposals come in all the time. We may have a fresh one already. Who knows?"

I know the fresh proposal he may be referring to.

No matter how great our relationship with Heath Mason has been over this past week, it was still just a proposal that brought us out here. He's still a client, and we're still subject to Agency rules. We're still his *curvas*, even though it feels like we're his partners now.

"We can't have another one already," I say. "We switched our profiles to temporarily unavailable, remember?"

"Shit, you're right," Josh says, "then let's get our phones switched on and alter that situation. Plus, our parents will be dying to hear from us, and Tiff will be ready to yap our ears off. It'll get us grounded."

His light-heartedness is returning, and so is mine. Me and Josh will be ok. He's right. And Heath will be sending us another proposal just as soon as we mark ourselves available. Definitely. He's been terrified of the negative spotlight for years, and I totally get it now. But we've made progress. *He's* made progress. Together. Long may it continue. Whatever that might entail.

I take my phone from my handbag, looking at its blank screen and trying to fathom how much of an impact this device makes on our lives, day after day without realising. It's insane.

"Ready to enter *real life* again?" I ask Josh, who's holding his in his hand, too.

He nods. "Let's do it. Three, two, one," he says, and we press the button.

I wonder what will be waiting for me as my phone fires up. Messages, voicemails, social media announcements, I imagine.

I ready myself for a load of *ping, ping, ping* vibrations, but there are so many notifications that they buzz through my whole fucking arm, and Josh's are the same.

I have to laugh, because hell, who'd have thought we'd have been quite so popular? We did say we'd be on a 'retreat' for a week, after all.

It's only when I examine my notification window that I see all the exclamation marks and missed calls. All the messages in capital letters, screaming. Ones from Mum, Dad, Tiff, Ebony…

WHERE ARE YOU?

WHAT THE FUCK, ELLA?? CALL US NOW!

CONNOR TOLD THEM, ELLA! HE TOLD THEM WHO YOU ARE!

I look at Josh and he's open mouthed, no doubt having the same stream of notifications as I'm having.

No.

No fucking way.

Connor can't have told them who I am. I can't be officially known as the ex who became a hooker and broke his heart. Not for real.

My fingers are shaking when I click on a link Mum has sent. I retch as I see the headline on one of the major news sites.

Connor Preston's 'hooker' ex revealed! Ella Edwards, 24, from Belgravia.

They have a picture of me, right there. A picture of me and Connor together, taken when we were teenagers alongside it. Then more. Pictures of me cheering him on at the side of a gig he was doing, staring up at him adoringly.

Oh fuck, how I get shivers, fingers trembling as I scroll.

The whole world knows who I am. They know ME, Ella – not Holly the whore – and they know I make money from fucking strangers.

"Holy fucking shit," Josh whispers when he sees the same photo I'm staring at.

Holy fucking shit doesn't cut it. It doesn't even come close.

I'm a viral fucking whore, who is being bitched about all over social media, and all over the fucking world.

Thanks Connor, you vile piece of shit. Thanks a fucking bunch. Like he hasn't hurt me enough already. I close my eyes and slam my head back against the headrest, trying to digest it.

I don't know what the fuck to do, so I turn to my boyfriend. I turn to Josh, who looks as though we're in the middle of a horror film – ghost faced, and open mouthed. He has no answers, just takes my hand in his and squeezes tight.

This means so much for us. For our lives, for our future, for our families and friends, for our anonymity, for our daily existence. For our jobs.

For our clients.

Even as I take deep breaths and ready myself for the utter shit storm ahead, there is one client in particular on my mind. Because there is no getting around the obvious question…

How the fuck are we ever going to see Heath again?

THE END

WANT MORE?

Did you enjoy your naughty week in Cannes?
If so, get ready for The Naughtiest List – available from November 27th 2025.

ACKNOWLEDGMENTS

As always, to John Hudspith, my editor. Goes without saying by now that you are such a key part of my novels, it's untrue. Thank you!

To Letitia, for the awesome cover. Thank you for nailing another Naughty.

To Sam, for your graphics and formatting – so often at extremely short notice.

To Nicole, at the very front of the reader line, with such valuable feedback, you're a dream.

To Emily, the ace at my side and an incredible project manager every single day, and to Misha, for jumping in to help whenever needed.

To my ARC Team, thank you all for reading The Naughty Week, and to all of the amazing readers out there expressing their enthusiasm and excitement for Ella's Naughty journey – as well as my other novels. I value every single one of you so much. I couldn't do this without you.

Same goes for my incredible family and friends. I hope you all know how loved and valued you are. Without you, I wouldn't be me. And the world wouldn't be nearly so *Naughty*.

ABOUT JADE WEST

First and foremost, I'm as filthy as my books suggest. There – got that one out of the way.

I am a total fantasist, living in the English countryside, with a great family and some amazing friends.

I'm epileptic, which has been quite a journey – still ongoing. Learning to live with disability when you're used to being independent is... hard. My support network is incredible, but I despise seizures and I miss my car. Badly. What I mean is, I miss freedom. Still, I have it easier than a lot of epileptics. I'm in no position to wail too loudly.

So, what else... I haven't grown out of being a goth since I was seventeen. Black velvet is my friend, along with glitter, long hair extensions, and Carl Jung.

I don't like tea or coffee, but I wish I did.

I love power ballads. A lot. I obsessively ruminate over lyrics, swimming in memories of the past as well as conjuring up projections for the future. So much for 'live in the now', because I don't do a great deal of it.

ABOUT JADE WEST

Oh, and I love books. Writing them, reading them, losing myself in imaginary realities. Can't get enough.

I'm best known for my novels Sugar Daddies, Bait, Call Me Daddy, and The Naughty List.

JOIN JADE ON SOCIAL MEDIA

www.facebook.com/jadewestauthor

www.facebook.com/groups/dirtyreaders

www.instagram.com/jadewestauthor

Tiktok - @jadewestauthor

Sign up to my newsletter via the website
www.jadewestauthor.co.uk

Printed in Dunstable, United Kingdom